The Vampire's Guide to Wooing a Scholar

Fated Vampire Mates, Book 2

Melissa Kendall

DRAGONBLADE PUBLISHING, INC.

ARE YOU SIGNED UP FOR DRAGONBLADE'S BLOG?

You'll get the latest news and information on exclusive giveaways, exclusive excerpts, coming releases, sales, free books, cover reveals and more.

Check out our complete list of authors, too!

No spam, no junk. That's a promise!

Sign Up Here

www.dragonbladepublishing.com

Dearest Reader;

Thank you for your support of a small press. At Dragonblade Publishing, we strive to bring you the highest quality Historical Romance from some of the best authors in the business. Without your support, there is no 'us', so we sincerely hope you adore these stories and find some new favorite authors along the way.

Happy Reading!

CEO, Dragonblade Publishing

Additional Dragonblade books by
Author Melissa Kendall

Fated Vampire Mates Series
The Vampire's Guide to Wooing a Dressmaker (Book 1)
The Vampire's Guide to Wooing a Scholar (Book 2)

The Seductive Sleuths Series
Companion to the Count (Book 1)
Mentor to the Marquess (Book 2)
Benefactor to the Baroness (Book 3)

For Janelle.
I wouldn't have finished this book without you.

Prologue

Paris, 1817

"WHAT DO YOU mean, you're *leaving?*" Marcus Deville asked as the Turkish rug beneath his feet seemed to pitch and heave like the deck of a ship. He couldn't possibly have heard her correctly.

The black-veiled woman standing in front of the smoldering fire in his drawing room rolled one of her billowing, gray silk sleeves up to the elbow, revealing pale skin mottled with deep-purple bruises. "I must."

Marcus sucked his teeth. "Who did that to you?" He would track them down and rip out their still-beating hearts with his bare hands. Despite all the terrible things Marguerite de la Valencia had done to him over the decades, he loved her as much as he resented her.

She restored her sleeve, then crossed the room and cupped his cheeks with ice-cold, skeletal fingers. "No one, my dearest."

His eyes burned with unshed tears as he took in the pallor of her face, her sharp cheekbones, and her sunken eyes. She'd once been so beautiful that emperors and kings had clamored for her attention. Now she looked like she belonged behind a glass case in a museum.

"Tell me what to do," he said in a hoarse voice.

She lifted her veil and pressed her lips to his forehead. "There is nothing to do." She pulled back and ruffled his short, light-brown hair. "Do not make the same mistake as I have and let atrophy consume you."

He swallowed past a lump in his throat. His maker, the woman who had been his lover and then his closest companion for more than a century, was dying, yet still she clung to her ridiculous stories.

She used her long, hooked nails to pluck a stray thread from the shoulder of the black, linen suit jacket his valet had selected for the evening's entertainment at the opera. "My sweet, logical Marcus." She toyed with the fabric of his snowy-white cravat. "There is nothing I could say that would convince you to begin searching for your mate, is there?"

Her voice was calm, but the way her green eyes deepened to a vibrant blue betrayed her growing anger. She was the dominant vampire in the nest and more than fifty years older than him. Even in her weakened state, she could kill him with a snap of her fingers.

He didn't care. Her fury at his insubordination was preferable to this unusual, almost-oppressive level of affection.

"There is not," he said. He would admit she was afflicted by some manner of illness that had stolen much of her strength over the past year, but the idea that the only cure was to find and form a bond with the singular individual who was fated to be her mate was absurd.

Fate had no place in the orderly, scientific world.

She unpinned his cravat, tugged it from his neck, then wrapped it around herself like a scarf. "You will believe, in time. I have already seen it." She twirled around the room with her arms spread. "She is a lovely woman, your mate. I could not have chosen a better match for you. I only wish you did not have to suffer so much before you find her." She sauntered over to a table, removed the stopper from a crystal decanter filled with thick, red liquid, and sniffed. "Animal again?" She pursed her lips. "Do you have anything more appetizing?"

He did not dignify her ominous premonition or her question with a response. First, she was always speaking in riddles, but nothing she had "foreseen" had yet come true. Second, she already knew the answer, even if she'd never understood his resistance to drinking from humans. Vampires, she often said, were predators. A wolf did not ponder the ethics of killing a sheep.

Except he had never wanted to become a wolf. She had thrust his condition upon him without his consent, turning a pacifist blacksmith into a soulless creature that had unceremoniously snuffed out the lives of dozens of men, women, and children in his village before his fledgling bloodlust had faded. Not that she cared. The few times he'd expressed his remorse and anger that she hadn't stopped his murderous rampage, she'd only laughed and called him sentimental.

"Please don't do this," he said. Begging her not to abandon him and his siblings was pointless—once she made a decision, she never changed her mind—but for the sake of his siblings, he had to try. The bond between maker and fledgling was stronger than parent and offspring. When others of their kind realized what had happened, there would be immediate petitions for Marcus's siblings to be absorbed by competing nests, as if they were spoils of war. To face those challenges and prevent his family from being torn apart, he would have to become as cold and ruthless as his maker.

She pranced back into his arms and took his hands. "Dance with me."

"Think about Jonathan," he said as he led her through the steps of a waltz. There was no music, but neither of them needed it after spending hundreds of hours in ballrooms across Europe. "He can't survive without you."

Marguerite had made five vampires after him, but young Jonathan was still dependent on his maker for feeding. Marcus feared what would happen when the rest of his family learned what she planned. Her icy detachment had united them for more than a century, reinforcing the strict hierarchy necessary for seven vampires to live in close proximity while also projecting an aura of strength that other nests feared.

Which made her current passivity even more unsettling. He would have preferred her to slice him apart with her nails or order him to walk into the sun. Instead, he was cradling her fragile frame as they danced beneath the flickering lights of a dusty chandelier.

She rested her head on his chest. "I am tired, Marcus. I wish to rest." She yawned. "You will watch over your brothers and sisters for me, won't you?"

He cupped the back of her head. "Of course."

She exhaled a soft breath, then sped out of the room in the blink of an eye.

Hours later, as he sat in a leather chaise drinking his fifth glass of wine, the double oak doors flew open and his younger brother staggered inside. Cordon's loose, brown hair was in disarray, his black, silk shirt was untucked, and he was missing a shoe. He was the third-eldest in the nest, but Marcus had never seen him look so devastated.

"She's gone," Cordon whispered. "Our maker is gone."

Marcus's first instinct was to rush across the room and envelop the taller man in his arms, but if the nest was going to survive, he would have to give up being the soft-spoken older brother who was always available for a reassuring smile and a hug. As the new head of the family, he needed to remain firmly in control. Then his siblings' vampiric natures would urge them to fall in line, order would be restored, and the risk of another nest declaring war on them would fade.

"I know," Marcus said.

Cordon ran a hand through his hair. "What are we going to do about Jonathan?"

Marcus swirled his wine around his glass. "We tell him the truth. There is no other option."

Tears dripped down Cordon's cheeks. He removed a scarlet handkerchief from his pocket and wiped them away. "I will do it."

Typical Cordon, always taking responsibility. Marcus was glad he was the eldest, as he couldn't imagine Cordon bearing the burden of authority. He would surely have taken every minor problem in the nest on his shoulders until he buckled beneath the pressure.

"No," Marcus said sternly. "That is my duty now. I will awaken him at sunset."

Then Jonathan would be less likely to go after Marguerite and they would have time to calm him down before sunrise. If it became necessary, Marcus could restrain him with blood shackles, but he did not enjoy using his power over his siblings. They were not a military unit.

They were a family.

And he intended for it to stay that way.

March 15th, 1867

To the Editor of *The Geographical Review*,

I must alert you to an egregious historical inaccuracy in volume no. 5 of your otherwise esteemed journal. Mr. Green suggests in 'On the Aleppo Incident' that residents of the doomed city were taken entirely by surprise by the earthquake of 1138, when it is well-established that several foreshocks the previous day caused many to flee preemptively.

If you wish to retain my subscription, I expect a retraction to be printed in the next issue.

Sincerely,
Miss Winifred Belltree

Chapter One

April 9th, 1867, Scotland

A s Marcus stood in front of the open door at the bottom of the north tower of the castle where he spent most of his waking hours, sweat beaded on his forehead and dripped down his face.

Coward.

A cool breeze curled around him, carrying the rich scent of the forest. He removed a silver flask from his pocket, unscrewed the lid, and filled his mouth with the thick, lukewarm liquid of concoction number twenty-seven. When he had swallowed every foul drop, he stepped forward until his boots sank in the mud and the wind dried the moisture on his skin.

A familiar tingling began in his fingers, followed by the rhythmic pounding of his pulse in his head. The moonlit trees reached for him with spindly arms and when he tilted his head up, the night sky was filled with twinkling stars that felt precariously positioned, as if at any moment, they would detach from the heavens and plummet to Earth, crushing him to dust.

Darkness crept into the sides of his vision. He wrenched his gaze down and focused on a single tree in the distance. It rushed toward him, barreling with the speed of a racing train. He threw his arms up to protect himself, but the impact never came. Someone grabbed him by the upper arm and jerked him backward. The next thing he knew, he was lying on the cold, stone floor of his workshop and looking up at a towering man with piercing-blue eyes and unnaturally sharp cheekbones.

It was his younger brother Cordon wearing an expertly tailored, black wool suit.

As Marcus shoved to his feet, he wiped the dirt from his hands on his brown twill trousers to keep Cordon from seeing how they trembled. "What are you doing here?"

It had been months since any member of his nest had visited. Not that he could blame them. Any affection his siblings had felt for him would have vanished after *that* disastrous day ten years ago when he had followed in their maker's footsteps and fled the nest. The most he could reasonably expect was a grudging respect, given his position as the eldest.

Cordon poked a key on a prototype of a writing machine sitting on a table next to a narrow window in the circular room. "Saving you, apparently. What were you doing out there, pretending to be a scarecrow?"

Heat crept up Marcus's neck. Rather than answer, he shoved past his brother and took a seat at his desk, where his journal was open to a fresh page. There was enough time to record the results of his latest experiment before sunrise. Unfortunately, the mixture of half cow and half pig blood was no more effective at staving off his attacks of nerves than any previous combination, as evidenced by Cordon's timely rescue.

He stabbed his pen back into its holder. A decade of tireless research, and he was no closer to a solution than the day he'd fled to the Scottish castle. A less determined man would have given up ages ago, but he refused to surrender while he had people to protect.

Even if they hated him.

"You should be out searching for your mate," Cordon said. "Not haunting this mausoleum."

Marcus slammed his journal shut. "I didn't think you cared."

"Atrophy might not manifest the way you expect, brother. After I recovered, I checked with other nests. Several vampires reported entirely different progressions from the bruising and fever I experienced."

Marcus leveled his best disapproving stare at his brother. "Do not presume to meddle in my affairs."

He had no desire to follow Cordon's lead. Only a few months earlier, his brother had compiled a list of scandalous activities to complete before he died of the mate atrophy he'd been suffering. During the execution of said list, he'd met his wife, Katherine, and the illness that had plagued him had vanished.

Marcus couldn't deny Cordon's miraculous recovery but refused to believe mating was the only solution. There had to be another cure, one that didn't require him to leave the castle or allow strangers to invade his sanctuary. Since drinking Katherine's blood had eased Cordon's symptoms prior to mating, Marcus was certain his solution would be found in the blood that sustained his kind's unnatural existence. It was the only possibility left he had not yet fully explored.

Cordon shook his head. "I should have expected you wouldn't take me seriously. Mating would require you to care about someone other than yourself."

"That's not fair."

It was also not true. Marcus loved each member of his nest so much that their absence in his life was like a festering wound in his heart. But he'd made a promise fifty years ago that he would do whatever it took to keep them together and no amount of pestering from his brother would steer him from that cause.

Cordon crossed the room and grabbed Marcus's upper arms. "Don't make the same mistake I made. I gave up searching, and it nearly killed me." His voice cracked. "I needed you, Marcus, and you *weren't there*."

A lump formed in Marcus's throat. He was extremely aware of the pain he'd caused by remaining in Scotland instead of flying to Cordon's side when his brother had insisted he'd been dying. Every part of him longed to beg for forgiveness, but that was not what Marguerite would have done. She would never have allowed a display of dominance from a vampire lower in the hierarchy than her to go unpunished. So even though he would have preferred to pull his brother into his arms and sob, he focused on the blood pumping through his body and willed it to gather in his shoulders. "Release me."

Cordon's eyes glowed a vibrant blue. "Not until you tell me why you ignored my summons."

"I couldn't leave my experiments." It was a lie, of course. The true reason was an unforgivable sin that burned in his stomach like hot coals. He could no longer leave the castle, even if he wanted to.

His brother scowled. "If our maker were alive, she would be ashamed."

Marcus bared his fangs, even as he mentally urged Cordon to stop. His brother was giving him no choice but to discipline him. "Release me before I am forced to *make* you."

"Do it," Cordon said, in a tight voice. "At least then I'll know I made you feel *something*."

Marcus sent his blood spiking out of his body, piercing Cordon like a hundred daggers. His brother uttered a strangled groan before collapsing to the ground. The crimson liquid staining his fine wool suit gathered into a pool, then crossed the floor and climbed Marcus's boots and re-entered his body through the pores in his skin. When every drop had returned, he crouched down and caressed his brother's hair.

"Do not question me again."

Cordon winced, but tilted his head to the side, bearing his throat. Submissive, at last.

Marcus helped his brother to his feet, then dismissed him with a wave of his hand. As Cordon scurried away, Marcus turned to the window. The moon sat high above the sprawling Scottish countryside, shining on a cluster of buildings. The village was far enough away that he couldn't make out individual structures, but could see the plumes of smoke rising from many chimneys.

A decade ago, he could have cooled his temper by taking a horse and riding into the woods to hunt. That was before his condition worsened. Now he couldn't even make it past the garden without collapsing.

He wasn't sure what was worse; knowing his siblings resented him as much as he resented Margurite or wishing desperately for their company—*any* company—regardless.

He ran a hand over his face. Dwelling on matters he couldn't easily change wouldn't help his situation. Better to distract himself with more mundane concerns. He picked up the pile of unread letters his housekeeper had left for him that evening.

The first three were of no consequence: requests from the few wealthy families who lived nearby to attend an evening of charades, a garden party, and a ball. He wondered how long they would solicit him before they gave up. It was almost enough to make him regret letting Cordon manipulate Queen Victoria into granting Marcus the title of the Earl of Kingsbury twenty years earlier. He'd never enjoyed altering the minds of humans, but it had been necessary to convince the queen into accepting the unofficial documents that had listed him at the time as a man of eight-and-twenty.

Back then, he'd craved the power that came with being a peer of the realm. That confident, covetous Marcus was a stranger to him now.

He tossed the invitations unceremoniously into the fire.

The fourth envelope, however, was addressed to one of his publishing companies. It should not have been routed to him. He tapped the stiff paper, debating its fate, before he cracked the wax seal and flattened the missive on his desk.

By the time he'd finished reading, he was smiling for the first time in longer than he could remember.

May 30th, 1867

Miss Winifred Belltree,

Your letter reached my desk by chance, but I am pleased to have received it. You have my sincere apologies that 'On the Aleppo Incident' was printed without thorough review. I have had the person responsible for accepting submission replaced to ensure it does not happen again.

As per your request, I have included the latest volume of *The Geographical Daily*, which includes a retraction. If you have other suggestions, I would be pleased to hear them.

Sincerely,
Kingsbury

Chapter Two

March 2nd, 1868, Toronto

WINIFRED BELLTREE DELICATELY lifted the corner of a yellowed page in the illuminated manuscript with two fingers and slid her thin, wooden page turner beneath. The hundred-year-old vellum crinkled and popped like her back after spending hours bent over a table in her family's library.

She gently flattened a vibrant illustration of an erupting Mount Vesuvius. It was no larger than her palm, but the detail was exquisite, from the thin lines of lava sliding down the mountain to the plumes of smoke rising into the sky. Choppy waves lapped the shore as three tiny figures huddled together outside the ruins of the destroyed city. She lifted the book toward her cousin and tilted it back and forth, making the gold leaf reflect the light of the sun shining through the window. "Isn't it lovely?"

"Beautiful," Winifred's cousin Felicity said. Felicity Sorrow, a twenty-year-old London debutante eager to take a break from the marriage market there, lounged on a maroon velvet settee with a copy of *The Night Side of Nature* held close to her face. Her lace gloves were tucked carelessly in her pocket, several black curls had escaped from her chignon, and one of her slippers was hanging from the toes of her right foot, ready to flop onto the thin carpet.

Winifred adjusted the spectacles perched on her nose and ignored the fact that her cousin hadn't actually looked up before responding, especially because Felicity had gifted Winifred the rare volume that had become her latest obsession. She still didn't know how her cousin had saved up enough of her pin money, or how she'd escaped from under the watchful gaze of the insufferably proper aunt who had accompanied her across the ocean from London for long enough to purchase the book, but she wasn't about to ask.

When one was fascinated by topics deemed inappropriate for ladies, one became adept at letting such mysteries go unsolved.

"Are you two almost done?" Felicity's older brother, Vincent, asked as he sauntered out from the rows of shelves with his hands shoved in the pockets of his black trousers, which were at least an inch too short. A casual observer might have mistaken him for Felicity's twin because of their matching height and raven hair, but there was an intensity to Vincent's brown eyes and a kind of repressed anger in his voice that made Winifred uneasy.

Or perhaps it was the ash falling from the end of the lit cheroot clenched between his teeth.

"Put that out," she said sharply.

"Anything you wish, my dear," Vincent said. He removed the abhorrent object from his lips and stabbed it into a half-empty glass of whiskey, then sprawled his lanky frame in the cushioned wicker chair next to hers.

Her arms erupted in gooseflesh, despite the red, wool shawl draped over her shoulders and the full-sleeved, printed pink cotton day dress beneath it. She scooted away from him, then glared at Felicity, who was still engrossed in her reading. Her cousin could have reprimanded her brother, but she refused to see anything but the best in him.

"I will never understand why you find those macabre tales so fascinating, Fel," she said, referring to the book in her cousin's hands. "The stories our parents told us were enough to give me nightmares."

From the time they'd been old enough to toddle, both girls had been taught how their Sorrow ancestors through Felicity's father and Winifred's mother had hunted impossible creatures. Felicity had embraced the learning, but Winifred refused to believe that there had ever been people who could transform into wolves or live forever by drinking the blood of innocents.

Her cousin flipped a page. "I could say the same for your obsession with natural disasters."

Winifred huffed. The difference was, the past tragedies she studied were fixed in time. Some interpretation was required, but disagreements could always be settled by returning to the original records. In contrast, Felicity's folk tales were fluid, evolving as each storyteller imparted their own biases to fit the narrative they wished to tell. A legend told a hundred years ago would bear little resemblance to its modern counterpart.

Winifred's stomach growled, reminding her it had been hours since breakfast. In fact, judging from the way the square of sunlight on the carpet had moved from one side of her desk to the other, it was nearly time for luncheon. She would have preferred a servant bring the meal to them, but that was foolish, not only because her parents had already warned her they did not approve of her spending so much time with her nose tucked in ancient texts, but also because her books were so fragile that even a single accidental crumb dropped onto a page could cause significant damage.

She returned the illustrated manuscript to the box she'd prepared to protect it from dust and light, then flexed the muscles of her stiff shoulders. "Shall we retire to the dining room?"

"Yes we should," Vincent said. "If we stay any longer, I'll start growing roots."

Felicity pressed her face into her book with a groan.

"I know," Winifred said. "But if we don't make occasional appearances, I fear my mother will tell Aunt Ethel to send you home early."

The two weeks Felicity had spent in Toronto had buoyed Winifred's spirits after her disastrous summer. Winifred was, admittedly, a little old to be unmarried, at two-and-twenty, but that didn't mean her parents needed to foist her upon every gentleman brave or foolish enough to approach them in public. It had become bad enough that she retreated to the library at any opportunity, even if it meant frequent criticisms from her mother about her bookish nature.

At least Felicity's presence had granted Winifred a brief reprieve. Her parents were so intent on ensuring the young woman enjoyed her stay that they were not paying as much attention to Winifred.

Unfortunately, Felicity could not stay forever. Soon she would return to London, and then Winifred would have to make do with communicating with her cousin through writing.

"A few minutes more," Felicity said. She put her book on top of a stack and returned to a normal sitting position. "I've been a terrible guest, making free use of our family's collection when I should have been helping." She put her elbows on her knees and her chin in her hands. "Have you compiled a list of candidates?"

It was Winifred's turn to groan. She'd come up with the idea of selecting a husband who would suit her needs that summer, after her mother had nearly blackmailed her into marrying a wealthy but foppish silk merchant. Such a match would have delighted most ladies but could not have been worse for Winifred. A young, ambitious husband would require his wife to join him at social events, entertain guests, and produce one or more heirs. Unlike other women who would have been eager to form such a pairing, Winifred despised crowds, had no talent for embroidery or music, and was deeply uncomfortable around children.

Vincent scoffed. "You are wasting your time. The only person Winifred will be marrying is me."

Felicity grinned. "What do you think, Winnie? We could be like sisters."

Winifred shuddered. Before her family had moved to Toronto, Vincent's infatuation had become so unbearable that she'd taken to keeping her father's hunting dogs at her side when he'd visited. For whatever reason, he despised the animals. She wished her father hadn't sold the hounds. The next-best defense she'd come up with was outright ignoring Vincent.

She stepped over his legs and joined her cousin on the settee, which was far enough away that he might not hear if she whispered. "I've hardly had time to compile a list. You've seen my mother. She insists on trotting me out like a prize mare at every event."

Felicity toyed with a loose thread in her gown. "At least you have parents. Uncle Ethan hardly knows I exist."

Winifred winced. "I'm sorry. I should have spoken with more care." After Felicity's parents died and Ethan Sorrow had become her guardian, she'd changed. Winifred distinctly remembered wondering why her once-energetic friend had started refusing invitations and tensing every time a suitor approached her at a ball for a dance. Felicity had denied anything was wrong, but the more Winifred had observed her cousin, the more she'd realized Felicity's behavior wasn't fear, but a kind of cautious anticipation. Like a street cat pressing itself to the ground and holding perfectly still while a mouse slowly crawled out from a hiding place.

"I forgive you," Felicity said. "Are there any other criteria you are considering?"

Winifred blew out a long breath. "I would like him to be kind. Intelligent. Most importantly, open-minded enough to allow his wife to pursue her own interests without being so poor that my parents would never approve."

There was one other criterion, but she did not dare speak it aloud while Vincent might hear. She hoped to find a husband who would allow her to rescue Felicity from the clutches of their uncle by hiring her as a companion.

Thus far, she'd failed to locate anyone who would suit. Possibly because she had restricted her search to other historians. Any man wealthy or powerful enough to be acceptable to her mother was invariably preoccupied with the acquisition of more wealth or power. If only she could meet someone who respected her love of research.

Except... she had. In a manner of speaking.

Several months ago, she had purchased the latest edition of a journal that had contained a well-written but inaccurate article regarding the Aleppo earthquake of 1138. Incensed by such flagrant disregard for historical fact, she had penned a complaint to the editor of the journal, which had miraculously been routed to the owner of the publishing company. His contrite response and follow-up retraction in the next issue had impressed her enough that she'd continued writing to him long after her grievance had been settled. It was terribly scandalous, given the intimate nature of their letters, and would have shocked her mother into a faint. From their correspondence, she judged he was well-read, empathetic, as devoted to the pursuit of knowledge as any proper scientist, and most importantly, unmarried.

She retrieved a letter from her pocket and flipped it around in her hands. "Well, there might be *one* man."

July 4th, 1867

Dear Winifred,

I hope the season was as uneventful as you wished and that you enjoyed the time you had with your cousin to the fullest. I must express my tremendous gratitude regarding your suggestion to use centrifugal force in my experiments. After some consideration, it occurred to me I could apply the same rotational force of a tornado through the construction of a machine. After months of failure, I am hopeful this newest invention will allow me to create more effective concoctions to treat my cattle.

Regarding your latest subject of research, I have attached a list of books that might suit your interests. Please inform me if you have difficulty acquiring them and I can make inquiries on your behalf to my suppliers.

Yours,
Marcus

Chapter Three

August 20th, 1867, Scotland

MARCUS HEFTED A cast-iron flywheel from his desk and carried it to where a half-constructed device waited, bathed in faint light shining through the single narrow window. He blew a wet clump of hair out of face as he lowered the wheel and slotted the square hole in its center into the shaft with a dull *clank*. Despite his hair being drenched in sweat, his throat was painfully dry. There was a pitcher of water within reach, but it would not quench his thirst.

He crouched and peered into the heart of the machine he had spent the last month creating, thanks to Winifred's advice. The problematic components were the central pinion and the bevel wheel it turned against. He had meticulously crafted both out of high-quality bronze, but the fitment wasn't close enough to ensure smooth operation. As a result, a bolt had loosened during his last experiment, causing several expensive glass vials in the latched spinning top of the machine to crack.

If his hypothesis was correct, the reason his concoctions failed to prevent his attacks was because the animal blood he used to create them possessed a component that inhibited healing. That would explain why when he mixed human blood with that of his livestock, the resulting compound formed clumps. As he had no intention of changing his diet, even if it meant remaining in seclusion forever, he needed to identify that toxin and remove it.

Unfortunately, separating blood into its constituent parts was proving far more difficult than he'd expected. By sheer chance, he'd discovered that agitation resulted in a subtle change in the appearance of his samples, but he'd yet to find a reliable method of producing this phenomenon without shattering his fragile glass vials.

"Damned thing," he whispered. He got onto his knees and peered into the motor. His fingers were too thick to move the delicate components. He reached inside until his thumb brushed over the bolt he needed to remove. Then a trembling started in his fingers and the bolt slipped out of his grip and dropped into a machine with a series of clinks.

What he needed was an assistant. Preferably one with smaller hands. He might have tried luring a maid into his workshop with the promise of higher wages, but he could not trust himself to behave in a gentlemanly manner when his vampiric instincts were so close to the surface. It was the same reason he kept away from his own kind; any vampire dominant enough to tolerate his presence would invariably discover his weakness and attempt a coup.

A soft knock provided a welcome distraction. He removed his grease-stained canvas apron, hung it on a peg on the wall, and opened the door to find a trembling maid with bright-red curls barely tucked beneath a bonnet standing in the hallway holding a domed tray in both arms.

"Y-Your evening meal, my lord."

He rubbed his temples with his thumb and forefinger. "Did Mrs. Grange instruct you to climb all the way up here to bring it to me?"

His foolishly eager new cook seemed determined to get him to consume her increasingly elaborate recipes. The only reason he'd hired her had been to feed his other servants and maintain the semblance of a normal estate. His body had not required human food in centuries, although he could tolerate it in small quantities.

The maid bobbed her head.

He could have told her to leave it on the floor, but then he risked the cook stomping up the many stairs to his workshop and smashing down his door. Better to indulge her and dispose of whatever she'd made some other way. Perhaps he'd wrap it up and bring it to the pigs.

He accepted the tray and waited for the maid to scurry around the corner of the spiral staircase before he glanced out the window. The slight tightening in his chest warned him he would have to rest soon. That was perhaps for the best, as his limbs were heavy with fatigue.

But when he returned to his bedchamber and saw what was waiting on his desk, a familiar fluttering started in his chest. He dug through the envelopes until he found the one he'd been waiting for, ripped it open, and read.

> *My dear Marcus,*
>
> *I hope you know how much I anticipate each of your letters. You are the only person I know who truly understands historical fact, even if your bent is more scientific. I have tried to express the importance of research to my parents, but they insist on preparing me for my future, as they see it.*
>
> *I have acquired the volumes you suggested and must thank you for such excellent selections. When I close my eyes, I can see the soot-filled sky, hear the roar of lava pouring down the mountain, and feel the soft kiss of ash landing on my skin. It is said some inhabitants of Pompei were engulfed with such speed that they remain where they perished, statues guarding the ruins of an ancient city.*

He chuckled as she went on about everything she'd learned from the books he'd recommended. She was as obsessed with natural disasters as he was with finding a way to prevent his attacks. Not that he'd told her the truth. She believed he was investigating a peculiar illness in his cattle that no one else had been able to identify. He was embarrassingly grateful for the twist of fate that had redirected her letter to his desk all those months ago. Corresponding with her was the only thing that had kept him sane, as the pleas from his brothers and sisters to rejoin them in London had intensified.

Yet she was risking far more. If anyone discovered their writing, the consequences to her reputation would be severe. He should have stopped long ago, but whenever he held one of her envelopes, it was like a different person took control of his body. In the rare moments when he was not consumed by his work, he acknowledged the awful truth: he wanted her to get caught. The cruel, jealous part of him that hated anyone able to move about in the world without being paralyzed by fear demanded he make others join in his suffering.

He swallowed through the pain in the back of his throat and continued to read.

> *Regarding your experiments, if your mixtures are not having the desired effect, the removal of heat might prove efficacious in enhancing the potency, or perhaps the addition of heat. Such methods have been used for millennia. The ancient Egyptians even heated herbs on bricks as a treatment for maladies of the lungs, as indicated by the Ebers Papyrus.*

That was an interesting idea. He had tried adding heat but had never considered the opposite. It would be challenging to maintain a consistent temperature, but perhaps if he constructed a miniature icebox in his laboratory…

Yes, that was worth pursuing. He ran his fingers over the slanted print. Once again, Winifred had proven helpful, despite him carefully concealing the exact nature of his experiments. It was terribly unfortunate her letters were delayed, as was necessary for post to travel from the newly established country of Canada. He could have benefited greatly from having her opinions much faster. For that reason, despite itching to jot down ways to apply her suggestions, he read through the rest of her letter, eager to see how he might help with her difficulties in exchange.

> *Furthermore, it seems that the crux of many of the concerns you have raised are rooted in a lack of assistance. I appreciate the mystique and solidarity of a lone scientist, but I cannot help but think you*

would benefit from a second pair of hands. When my cousin visits, she allows me to prattle on at length, even though she is entirely uninterested in history. Her company has proved very useful in helping me focus. Is there, perhaps, someone you could invite into your laboratory to sit while you work?

He sighed. He wished it were as easy as she suggested. The last time he'd attempted to hire another scientist, he'd ended up losing his patience and scaring the man into fleeing the castle in the dead of night.

I admit, my cousin's presence this month has been all that has kept me from tearing out my hair in frustration. My parents have grown even more insistent in their demands that I find a husband. They do not understand the value of my research and have threatened to close up the library and sell the books if I am not wed by the end of the year.

He rubbed his thumb over a dark splotch on the paper as he imagined her heartbreak when her parents presented her with the ultimatum she described. As the daughter of newly wealthy textile merchants, she would be expected to marry well, preferably to one of the few titled men in Canada.

A future he'd placed in turmoil through their correspondence.

His thoughts came to a sudden halt as the solution to both of their problems hit him like a punch to the stomach. What he needed was someone to keep him from slipping into despair, an assistant who was sufficiently submissive that his vampire half would not see them as a threat while also being brave enough to endure his occasional bursts of temper.

None of his previous assistants had lasted because they had all been men.

In exchange for Winifred filling the role, he could offer the escape she so desperately desired. Given what she'd said about her parents, he guessed they'd give up their daughter if it meant achieving the social connections they wanted. It was so obvious, he couldn't believe he hadn't thought of it before.

He scrambled for a sheet of vellum and began laying out their future in ink.

Chapter Four

September 12th, 1867, Toronto

"ARE YOU EVER going to tell us the name of your mysterious suitor?" Felicity asked as she flipped through the pages of yet another occult manuscript. Winifred assumed it would soon join the teetering stack beside the upholstered mustard velvet divan Felicity had occupied with her brother for most of the morning. It was one of many battered, mismatched pieces of furniture that Winifred's mother had banished to the library for being too hideous to allow guests to see.

"I might," Winifred said. She tapped her slipper-clad toes on the carpet and tried to focus on the tiny print in the textbook lying on the table in front of her, but she felt as tightly wound as a clock spring. It had been several weeks since she had reluctantly admitted she had a gentleman in mind as a potential husband, and every moment of that time had been spent with both Felicity and Vincent nipping at her heels for information. She hadn't intended to offer them further details—a lady needed *some* secrets of her own—but Marcus's latest letter had come as such a shock that she felt she would burst unless she told someone.

She removed an envelope from her pocket and held it out to her cousin. "Here."

"What's that?" Vincent asked. He reached out and would have snatched the item from Winifred's hand if it weren't for Felicity swatting him like a misbehaving dog.

"Not for you," she said. Then she took the letter and unfolded it. Winifred stood behind her cousin and leaned over her shoulder as she read.

Winifred,

Please forgive my frankness, but I have come to the startling realization that our problems are complementary. You need a husband who will allow you free rein to pursue your interests, and I require a competent assistant. If you are amenable to an arrangement, it would be my pleasure to have you as my wife. You have my solemn vow as a member of the House of Lords, and as a gentleman, that I will never impose upon you any duties beyond those required to avoid scandal. Anything you desire, I shall provide.

Yours,
Marcus

Felicity's eyes widened. "Marcus Deville? The Earl of Kingsbury?"

Vincent straightened. "You're in contact with that misanthrope? You refer to him in such an informal manner of address?"

Winifred's cheeks heated. "We have been corresponding for months."

"Where did you meet him?" Vincent asked sharply. "Does your mother know?"

"I haven't, and no," Winifred said. "One of my letters was redirected to him by mistake, and he responded. In any case, I am quite certain Mother will overlook the impropriety if I become a countess."

Felicity frowned. "Oh, cousin, what if he is an absolute brute?"

Winifred clasped her hands on her lap. The concern in Felicity's voice made her throat tighten, cutting off the defense she desperately wanted to raise for Marcus. Even though she had never heard his voice or seen his face, she could not believe a man who wrote with such eloquence could be a 'brute.' In any case, it was not as if she'd had much success finding an appropriate suitor in Toronto. She had not yet broached the topic of keeping Felicity with her as a companion to Marcus, but she felt confident he would be amenable to her request. At least he had promised to allow her to continue her research. That alone was worth whatever cost he demanded.

"Tell me you are not seriously considering his proposal," Felicity said.

Before Winifred could respond to that, the door to the library flew open and her mother stormed inside. Mrs. Belltree's black hair was confined in a tight bun at the back of her head, her light-blue eyes were narrowed, and her thin lips were pinched.

"M-Mother," Winifred said. "We were just about to join you."

Mrs. Belltree crossed her arms. "Do not lie to me, child. You have been spending far too much time sequestered in this dusty room. I understand your desire to entertain Felicity, but you must resume your search for a husband at once. I do not wish to see you become a spinster."

An ache began between her temples. It wasn't as if she hadn't *tried*, but any suitor who spent more than a few minutes in her presence always found a reason to flee after hearing her lecture about the Destruction of Antioch or the Calcutta cyclone.

She couldn't help it. Men, with their appraising glances and disingenuous flattery, made her nervous. The only one not related to her with whom she'd ever held a meaningful conversation had been Marcus, and that hardly counted, as his responses took several weeks to arrive, which gave her plenty of time to organize her thoughts.

Felicity shoved to her feet. "I apologize, Aunt. It is as much my fault as Winifred's that we have not attended events the last several nights."

Vincent curled his lip. "Perhaps it is time for us to return home, sister."

"No!" Winifred cried. When both Felicity and her mother looked at her, she flushed. "I-I mean… It is not Felicity's fault. Do not punish her for my failure. It is only that my research—"

"*Research!*" Mrs. Belltree threw her arms in the air. "That is all you care about. Yet unlike your cousins, you refuse to educate yourself on our family history."

Of course her mother would raise that argument, even though it had been Mrs. Belltree who had agreed to Mr. Belltree's demand to relocate after Winifred had returned one night from her uncle's home with their family crest branded between her collarbones, the result of a barbaric tradition.

Her mother huffed. "I have been more than patient, Winifred. If you cannot secure a husband by the end of the month, you *will* accept Vincent's offer, even if I have to burn every book in this library."

Her mother's threat combined with Vincent's self-satisfied smirk shattered the last of Winifred's restraint. Becoming the wife of her despicable cousin would be worse than imprisonment, even if it pleased Felicity. She straightened her shoulders. "The Earl of Kingsbury has asked me to marry him."

Vincent paled. "Impossible."

Mrs. Belltree's jaw dropped before she snapped her mouth shut and beamed. "Oh, why didn't you say so?" She rushed forward, toppling over several stacks of books. "Tell me more about the earl," she said as Vincent stormed out of the room. She clasped Winifred's hands. "Has he recently come to town?"

Winifred swallowed thickly. "No, Mother. He, ah… is in Scotland."

Mrs. Belltree tilted her head. "Scotland?" She glanced at Felicity. "If this is a joke you girls have conjured, I do not find it amusing."

Winifred wanted nothing more at that moment than to crawl beneath the settee and curl into a ball, but her mother had her hands in a tight grip.

She had no choice. Her mother would scrutinize any excuse she made up, and she had never been adept at lying.

It would have to be the truth.

"He responded to a letter I sent some months ago regarding an article in a magazine."

Her mother's face turned a startling shade of purple. "And you have been in contact all this time? My dear, you are not yet betrothed!"

This was the part that would be difficult to explain, but Winifred hoped the offer of marriage would be enough to make her mother overlook any impropriety. "Yes. He had some interesting theories on how to better predict earthquakes based on the movement of tidal currents." She stopped there, even though returning to the subject of her interest made her want to go on for hours. Talking to her mother about her recent discoveries would do nothing to help her situation, though.

The deep lines on Mrs. Belltree's face eased. "Well, you cannot continue behave so improperly if you are to be a countess."

She dropped Winifred's hands. "I should have guessed you would find a bookish suitor. But at least he has a title." She beamed. "This is excellent news. I will speak to your father at once."

"So eager," Felicity said, after Mrs. Belltree had left. "If we're lucky, maybe she'll book passage on the same ship as Aunt Ethel."

Winifred ran her fingers over the folded edges of Marcus's letter. It was happening. If things went according to plan, soon she would be settled far from her managing parents, with Felicity at her side. She wouldn't have to promenade in front of suitors for hours each night, dressed in gowns that made her skin itch and her chest ache. She would have everything she wanted.

All she had to do was marry a man she'd never met.

Chapter Five

October 30th, 1867, Scotland

M ARCUS PULLED BACK the edge of a velvet curtain in his workshop as a cloud passed across the sun. He should have been with his valet preparing for the wedding, but he could not resist attempting to catch a glance of his bride-to-be as she arrived. He'd spent the past several weeks imagining what it would be like to see her for the first time. Perhaps he would wait for her family to retire to their assigned rooms and then surprise her by appearing from one of the secret passages. She would spin around, her lips parted, her unruly hair tied tightly behind her head, her spectacles falling down her nose.

He released the curtain and returned to his worktable. The hours until the ceremony were passing with agonizing slowness. If he did not occupy his mind, he would end up so nervous that he would suffer another attack and fail to speak his vows. He'd already sent his valet away twice because Marcus could not step a foot outside his tower without feeling as if he were going to faint.

There was a loud knock on his door.

"Let me in," an irritated voice said.

Cordon again. Marcus allowed his brother inside. Unlike the last time he'd visited, he looked at Marcus with an expression so grave that he half-expected his brother to tell him one of their siblings had died.

"Come to offer congratulations?" Marcus asked weakly.

"Lucina sent me." Cordon palmed a glass paperweight from atop a pile of papers on Marcus's desk and rolled it around in his hands. "She wanted me to tell you several vampires were killed in Glasgow last week. There are rumors that hunters have returned to Scotland."

Marcus straightened. "That's impossible." He trusted Lucina, his youngest sister and the leader of the ancient vampire council known as the Wild Hunt, but she had to be mistaken. "There hasn't been a hunter sighting here in over a century."

The humans known as hunters had once reigned over the Continent with an iron grip, dispatching any vampire that was unlucky enough to stumble across their path. The Wild Hunt had been formed to address the hunter threat; by limiting how many humans could be turned, the number of fledgling vampire attacks decreased until the hunters eventually faded into obscurity.

"Then you will do nothing," Cordon said.

Something about the way his brother had said that made Marcus bristle. "There is nothing to be done." He turned to the window. "Lucina is mistaken."

He clenched his hands and forced himself to breathe slowly as the walls shivered around him. There could be no hunters, because if there were, every member of his nest was in danger while he remained stuck in his castle like a coward.

"Do you intend to turn Miss Belltree?" Cordon asked.

"Eventually," Marcus said. "She will need time to adjust to the idea."

He didn't want to consider what he'd do if she reacted poorly. There was always his eldest nest sister, Seraphina, who could erase human memories, but there would still be the problem of Winifred being his wife.

"You should cancel the wedding," Cordon said suddenly. "You hardly know Miss Belltree. It could be a trap."

Marcus did not dignify that comment with a response. In reality, he knew more about Winifred than his own siblings. He knew she struggled with crowds and loud noises, that she always slept on her side, and that she was equally excited and anxious for their upcoming union. Instead of talking to his brother, he should have been finding her and easing her worries. He could only imagine how terrified she must be, preparing to become the wife of a man she had never seen. She would be second-guessing her choices even now. Any rational woman would be.

"She's not who you think she is," Cordon said.

"Of course she isn't," a tall, black-haired man wearing a baggy sack coat said as he swaggered into the room from behind Cordon. "All women are tricksters."

Marcus's pleasure at seeing his youngest brother, Jonathan, for the first time in months was so overwhelming that he almost enveloped the man in a hug before remembering that Marguerite would never have done anything of the kind. Instead, he inclined his head. "It is good to see you, Jonathan."

"Do not tell me you missed me." Jonathan put his hands in his pockets, looking around as if evaluating the small space the way he might assess a museum or a bank vault. He was one of the most accomplished thieves in all of Europe, in part because he could walk into a business three times wearing a different disguise and never be recognized.

"Have you come to warn me not to marry Miss Belltree as well?" Marcus asked.

Jonathan walked over to the fireplace and picked up a cigar from a box on the mantel, which he twirled in his fingers. "Certainly not. If you want to chain yourself to a woman and face questions as to why you never age or venture out during the day, I won't stop you." Then he turned, still flipping the cigar. "Marcus is the eldest, Cordon. It's not our place to tell him what to do."

"He is making a mistake," Cordon said, in a tight voice.

Jonathan lifted one eyebrow. "You've got that right. He should be out enjoying his last hours as a bachelor, not sitting here chatting."

Cordon snatched the cigar out of Jonathan's hands. "Will you take nothing seriously?"

Marcus edged between the two vampires and shoved them

apart. "Enough."

Their problem was a lack of structure. His absence in their daily lives meant there was no dominant vampire in the hierarchy. Without consistent orders, their bickering would escalate to a power struggle that one of them would not survive. He had to redirect their energy to more productive efforts.

He clasped Cordon's shoulder. "I will not jeopardize the safety of the nest without proof. If you believe the hunters have returned, then bring me evidence."

His brother dipped his head. "As you command."

"As for you, Jonathan," Marcus said. "Observe my guests and inform me if you notice anything suspicious." Then he waved a hand, and both brothers vanished. Not a moment too soon, as their squabbling had become tiresome. He was too nervous about his upcoming nuptials to be settling conflicts, even if it made him feel rather nostalgic for when they had all lived together in Paris. He could have that again, if only he could find a way to manage his attacks. Now that Winifred had arrived to assist him, he would have a second pair of hands to help with his experiments.

Winifred.

Months of anticipation and she was finally within reach.

According to his duty as host, he should have greeted his visitors at the door as they'd arrived, but he feared if he faced them when his nerves were so rattled, he would suffer another attack.

Meeting Winifred alone, however, might be manageable.

His valet would be irritated by the further delay in preparing for the ceremony, but Marcus could no longer wait. He ran down the tower steps and then along the hall until he reached the room his housekeeper had assigned to her. But when he lifted his fist, he heard a voice. Instead of knocking, he ducked into the adjoining room and moved the dusty bookshelf to reveal a secret passageway that ran parallel to several of the rooms on the floor. He had not intended to spy, but he could not resist the urge to see her, if only for a moment.

He squeezed through the narrow, cobwebby space until he'd reached a peephole, then peered through and sucked in a breath.

She was standing directly in front of him.

His heart fluttered in his chest. She had the exact uncontrollable, brown, curly hair he'd imagined, tucked into a braid that looked ready to burst apart at any moment, and wide, brown eyes framed by thick eyelashes hidden behind wire-rimmed spectacles perched on her nose.

He'd expected her to be with a lady's maid, but she was alone. Her slim figure was draped in a loose-fitting cream silk dressing robe and a long, white dress lay draped over the length of her bed, along with a pair of white slippers and a sheer veil.

"Oh, Marcus," she said.

He startled, smacking his shin against the wall. Hearing her say his given name in such a breathy voice made his skin erupt in gooseflesh.

She was thinking about him.

Then she walked back to the bed, sat down, and let out a heart-wrenching sob.

The posture stabbed at Marcus's heart. She looked so vulnerable. Terrified. And it was all his fault. He reached for the clasp to open the wall when there was a knock at her door. She wiped her tears away with a handkerchief she'd pulled out of her sleeve. "Come in."

An older woman wearing an elaborate, light-green gown with wide, puffed shoulders and a cinched waist entered. She shared Winifred's dark hair and large, brown eyes, which could only have meant she was Mrs. Belltree.

"Terribly rude of your new husband not to greet us," Mrs. Belltree said. Instead of comforting her daughter, she swept across the room and scrutinized Winifred's wedding dress. "And this evening wedding! Such an unusual man." Her brows drew together. "It is almost as if he's..."

Marcus stiffened. Had he been discovered so soon? That would be disastrous, given his inability to leave the castle.

"It's almost as if he's what?" Winifred asked.

Mrs. Belltree shook her head. "It matters not. The man is eccentric, but he is still an earl."

Marcus forcibly relaxed his muscles. He was safe, for the moment.

Mrs. Belltree picked up the garment on the bed by the shoulders and held it to her own body. "Do not fret, my dear. I remember the day I married your father. I was in quite a similar state."

Winifred put her knees to her chest and wrapped her arms around them. He cursed Mrs. Belltree for arriving before he could enter and tell Winifred that his intentions were honorable. She didn't need a lecture; she needed reassurance that she wasn't about to marry a monster.

It wasn't entirely Mrs. Belltree's fault, his conscience reminded him. He'd already have been introduced to Winifred if he'd done his duty properly.

"Well, get up, child," Mrs. Belltree said.

Winifred shoved her balled-up handkerchief away. "What?"

Mrs. Belltree tutted. "You know the Sorrow family custom. This is the way things have always been. I have also prepared the other items you will require..."

Marcus quickly shuffled away. As curious as he was to get a better look at Winifred, he would not impose upon her any more than he already had. He edged out of the secret passage, dusted the cobwebs from his trousers, then grimaced. He had a mere hour before he was expected in the ballroom, where they would marry. That would have to be enough time for his valet to prepare him.

He wanted Winifred to have the best possible first impression.

Chapter Six

WINIFRED SAT AT the foot of a bed in an unfamiliar room with her head in her hands as her stomach gurgled and the stale oatcakes she'd eaten that morning threatened to rise. Not once during the ocean crossing had she expected her wedding to be so stressful. Despite weeks of anticipating this moment, she felt as if she'd been dropped into the situation entirely unprepared. That her future husband hadn't met them at the door made her even more nervous. What if he had changed his mind and would spurn her at the altar?

It was an absurd thought, as such an action would result in a terrible scandal, but she couldn't seem to convince herself that it wasn't going to happen.

Oh, God, she was about to *marry* a man she'd *never met*.

It was not a future she'd ever seriously imagined for herself, even though such matches were not uncommon. She had, in fact, barely considered what marriage would be like until recently. It had been much easier to envision a life focused on research and the eventual companionship of her cousin. Now she was in Scotland, becoming the wife of a man who would have nearly as much, if not more, control over her than her parents had ever had.

She dropped her hands from her face. There was no point in moping. If Marcus kept his word, she would soon be free of her managing mother and ready to begin her new life. She would simply have to force herself to endure standing in a crowded, noisy room for an hour. This was not the first time she'd had to smile and nod while screaming inside her head.

She smoothed the fabric of her gown, which had become slightly wrinkled from her terrible posture. At least the garment was lovely, made of ivory silk moire with a white tulle veil. The bodice had puffed sleeves trimmed with white knitted lace. For jewelry, her mother had generously gifted her an opal-and-seed-pearl pendant in the shape of a sun on a gold necklace with matching teardrop earrings. It was strangely comforting wearing her family crest, even though the same symbol was burned into her flesh between her collarbones, the last gift her uncle had given her before she'd left England.

She checked her coiffure one last time in the small mirror above the writing desk and then lifted her chin and strode with confidence she did not feel into the hallway, where her father was waiting. Her feet seemed to sink into the floor as she realized how much he'd aged in the past year. The silver strands in his hair had multiplied tenfold. The slim-fitting silver coat he wore made him appear almost sickly thin, and when he turned to her and smiled, there were noticeably more dark spots on his wrinkled cheeks.

"It is not too late to change your mind," he said as she placed her fingers on his arm. "You could still accept that scoundrel Vincent's offer." His tone was serious, but his wide smile gave him away. She responded by "accidentally" stepping on his toes.

"I almost wish I'd been kidnapped by pirates," she said. At least *then* she'd have some idea what to expect.

He squeezed her arm. "Are you sure about this?"

She kissed his cheek. "Yes."

A chance to achieve her dream of becoming an esteemed scholar was worth the risk of venturing into foreign territory, and far better than being shackled to a man whose presence made her nauseated.

"Wait until you see the earl," her father said, when they arrived at the dining hall. "I've never seen such fearsome scars, and an eyepatch, too. All he is missing is a parrot on his shoulder. You might yet get your wish."

She stomped on his foot again. Not that it stopped the old man from laughing.

A strangled laugh drew Winifred's attention to her cousin Felicity, dressed in her white bridesmaid's dress. When Felicity met Winifred's gaze, she grinned and waved. A small gesture, but it settled Winifred's nerves more than anything her mother had said.

"Thank you," Winifred whispered as her father led her toward the door. She wished Felicity could have joined her while she'd prepared, but Mrs. Belltree had insisted that an archaic Sorrow family tradition required that the mother of the bride solely perform the task.

"Ready?" Winifred's father asked.

She licked her dry lips, then nodded.

The doors opened, revealing a small crowd sitting in rows in front of a friendly-looking man she assumed was the vicar. Her mother was there, of course, along with Aunt Ethel. Uncle Ethan was noticeably absent, along with Felicity's brother, Vincent.

Winifred did not miss them.

The remaining guests were unfamiliar, two men Winifred assumed were related to Marcus. Both were tall, with unusually pale skin and dark hair, but their countenances could not have been more different. The man closer to her looked as if he'd bitten into a lemon; his lips were pressed into a tight line and his bright, blue eyes were wide. The other man wore the slack, bored look of a parishioner impatiently waiting for the end of a lengthy sermon.

Then Winifred saw Marcus, and time stood still.

He was shorter than she'd expected, although broad of shoulder, with unfashionably long, brown hair, startlingly pale skin, and a nose of extraordinary proportions. He held his arms stiffly at his side while rocking back and forth slightly on his feet, looking as if he'd rather have been anywhere else in the world.

It was that last detail that gave her the strength to step forward when he met her gaze and an electric heat shot through her. His eyes widened and his finely shaped lips spread into a grin. She hardly noticed her father drawing her forward, because all that mattered was Marcus, and the warmth in his expression. Nor did she remember the words her father whispered as he handed her to her new husband. Later, all she would recall from the few minutes she spent next to Marcus was feeling his boney arm beneath her fingers and the way he gently cupped her cheeks with his ice-cold hands before pressing a feather-light kiss to her lips.

There was some business with signing a contract with witnesses before her mother ushered her into a cavernous room decorated lavishly with roses, now a married woman, surrounded by chattering family members yet feeling completely alone. She twirled the simple gold band wrapped around her finger. According to the books on ceremonies she had read, she should have been bustled into a carriage and taken to her new home. That, of course, had not been necessary, as the wedding had taken place at her new home, but it left her scrambling to determine etiquette. Should she be speaking to her guests? Standing next to her new husband? Arranging the opening of her bridal trousseau?

Then she spotted Felicity in the crowd, clutching a lace fan as she moved through the room. When she spotted Winifred, she changed direction. They met with a clasping of hands.

"I'm so glad to—"

"You look—"

They stopped and blinked before bursting into giggles, which Winifred stifled. She was a married woman now. A countess. It was entirely inappropriate to be so energetic while there were guests for her to entertain.

"I'm sorry I didn't come see you sooner," Felicity said. "Aunt Ethel wouldn't let me leave my room until the ceremony, as a punishment." She grinned. "I might have engaged in some gambling on the ship."

Winifred giggled, then squeezed her cousin's hands. "Thank you for coming. I will ask him about hiring you as soon as I can."

Felicity squeezed back. "You are a true friend." Her thin eyebrows drew together. "I admit, I didn't actually expect you to go through with this marriage. The earl is an excellent match, of course, but..." She glanced around, then leaned closer. "Do you not find his complexion rather strange, Winnie? The man is as pale as a ghost."

Winifred tilted her head. "He is a scientist, Fel. He spends most of his time engaged in research."

"Then what about his brothers? They are equally as pallid."

"That is enough," Winifred said. The words came out more sharply than she'd intended. She was rather tired of listening to criticism about her husband. Her parents had spent much of the journey complaining about Marcus's insistence on a small, late-night ceremony. They would not refuse him, given his status, but they were not above gossip. Her mother had speculated the earl was either weak of constitution or so miserly that he refused to spend any more than necessary on the wedding. Winifred had not enjoyed hearing such talk, especially when it seemed at odds with the Marcus she thought she knew.

Not that scientists couldn't also be pinchpennies, but she had difficulty reconciling his descriptions of an enormous library with her parents' speculations.

Felicity's lips thinned. "I worry for you, Winnie. Your new husband..." She lowered her voice. "Something is not right about him. He is an *earl*. Why would he offer to marry you when there are dozens of ladies within arm's reach?"

Winifred shook her head. "I appreciate your concern, but it is unnecessary." She forgave her cousin's worries in part because they reminded her of something that had slipped her mind until that moment. Marcus's letters. The ones he'd sent since she'd accepted his proposal. If Felicity had read them, she'd understand there was a genuine connection between Winifred and the earl.

Not love, of course, but fondness.

Her spectacles fogged as she remembered the soft press of Marcus's lips. Her attraction to him was entirely unexpected, but not unwelcome. If she was going to spend the rest of her life at his side, then some level of affection would ease their path, even if their partnership was one of convenience.

Felicity tucked her arm in Winifred's and led her around the room. "Well, if you are quite certain. Remember that I am only a letter away if you discover anything about the earl that makes you fear for your life."

Winifred could not help the laugh that burst out of her lips. "Fear for my *life*? I think not, cousin. Even if such a thing happened, we are now man and wife. There would be little recourse." That fact should have been terrifying, but Winifred had reassured herself of her safety on the long trip by reading Marcus's letters over and over until she could recite them from memory.

"There is one thing that concerns me, though," Winifred said. She lowered her voice. "The wedding night."

She had read about the act of intercourse, but the few texts in her parents' library had only referred to it in vague terms. The books on animal husbandry had been more enlightening, but after exploring her own body with her fingers, she had difficulty imagining how a man would insert himself in such a narrow channel.

Then again, would Marcus even want to engage in such activities with her? He'd assured her in his letters that he did not require an heir, and she had no intention of becoming pregnant, thanks to a special tea she'd learned how to brew from a book.

"I don't know how—" Felicity started before Marcus appeared in front of them. Without him having to ask, Winifred released her grasp on her cousin and offered the earl her hand. He took it, placed it on his sleeve, and pulled her tightly to his side. This happened so quickly and without a single word spoken that when Winifred peered over her shoulder, Felicity was scowling.

Winifred mouthed an apology before returning her attention

to her husband. Even through the fabric, his arm was quite cold. She shivered.

"I've grown tired of socializing," he said, in a voice so deep, it nearly made her swoon.

"Me, too," she said, and it was true. She'd barely slept the previous night, and the sound of so many people speaking and shouting combined with the scent of roses and the tight clasp of her wedding gown made her want to wriggle out of her skin.

"Come," he said, tugging her toward the exit. "No one will miss us."

This was it. Her husband was taking her away. Anyone remaining in the room would assume he intended to deliver her to her maids. She chewed the inside of her cheek. Her mother had given her very little preparation for what was to come, telling her only that there might be some pain and that Winifred should lie silently and wait for it to end. That conversation had done nothing to ease her fears. So, as Marcus led her up the stairs, the fluttering inside her chest intensified until she nearly tripped over her own feet. She was about to ask him to slow down when he stopped in front of her door and cleared his throat.

"Do you, er, like my castle?"

The way he rubbed his hands together and bit his bottom lip eased her fears. However uncomfortable she felt, this was Marcus, not a complete stranger.

"It's lovely," she said. Which was true. The plain, stone walls and lack of gaslights or candles might have been unnerving to some, but she had never been intimidated by darkness.

Monsters that were not afraid to show themselves in the light of day were far more terrifying than those who preferred to remain concealed.

"Good." He tugged at his cravat. "Good. Well. If there is, ah, anything you require, you need only ask my—*our*—housekeeper, Mrs. Gillanders."

Then, before she could raise the subject of Felicity or anything else, he turned around and left her standing there, staring openmouthed at his retreating form.

Chapter Seven

MARCUS SCRAPED HIS tongue with his teeth as he made his way to his tower, but a bitter taste clung to the inside of his mouth like sticky toffee. Nothing was going according to his plans. He'd mentally played out the events of this day a hundred times, but precisely zero of those scenarios had involved him abandoning his new wife on his wedding night.

One moment he'd been standing in front of Winifred, feeling like a sailor rowing toward land he had been charting for months. The next moment, a prickling sensation had started in his feet and swept up his body until it had filled his head with static. Rather than allow her to see him experience an attack, he'd taken the easy route and fled.

Coward.

It shouldn't have bothered him. Winifred had accepted his proposal because it served her interests as much as his own. He was a scientist, and she was a historian. Their lives had no room for anything else.

He ascended the spiral steps to his tower three at a time, then flew inside and slid down the closed door and wrapped his arms around his knees. Before Winifred had arrived, it had been easier to pretend everything was fine. It didn't matter that he missed his siblings because he kept busy with a search for an alternative to mating. There was no need to hunt when livestock fulfilled his need for blood.

But he couldn't lie to himself forever. His condition was

worsening at an alarming rate. The Marcus of a year ago would never have avoided interacting with his guests because he didn't want to face that prickling, panicky sensation again.

Coward.

He slowly uncurled his limbs and forced himself upright, then descended the steps to the bottom floor and the exit that led to the forest behind the castle. It was nothing more than a hunk of wood and metal, but he would have preferred to be staked through the heart or drowned in the ocean rather than cross through it. He could no longer even think about grasping the handle without feeling like the walls were closing in on him.

"There you are," a chipper voice said.

Marcus turned to see Jonathan leaning against the wall at the bottom of the steps. His baggy sack coat was unbuttoned, revealing an equally shabby mismatched waistcoat and trousers.

"I am not sure if I should offer congratulations or condolences," Jonathan said.

Marcus rubbed his aching back. After the attack outside Winifred's room, he felt as anxious as Cordon had seemed when he'd delivered Lucina's message. At least he had no fear of receiving a lecture from his youngest brother. Jonathan could be dangerously reckless when it came to protecting anyone he cared about, and his youth meant he often let his temper get the better of him, but he was the least inquisitive person Marcus had ever met.

"I was going to watch for movement in the forest," Marcus said, even though Jonathan hadn't asked. "In case Cordon is right and there are hunters nearby."

Jonathan removed a cigar from inside his jacket and twirled it in his fingers. "Do you want me to flush them out?" His grin widened as he stuck the end of the cigar between his teeth. "I could be the bait."

Marcus chuckled. That was typical Jonathan, always itching for a fight. Here, however, a more subtle plan was warranted. "No. Not yet."

Jonathan curled his lip in obvious disappointment.

Marcus sighed. Without instruction, his brother was likely to get himself into trouble. How much longer would it be before every member of his nest came to him for orders? He should have been alarmed, but it felt right to be in charge again, like things were back to how they'd been after Marguerite had left, but before Marcus had let his pride get the better of him.

"Keep watching my guests," Marcus said. It was possible that Lucina's warning and the Belltrees' arrival were unrelated, but it was too much of a coincidence not to investigate. "Tell me if any of them leave the grounds."

Jonathan lifted one eyebrow. "Even your pretty new wife?"

An image of Jonathan embracing Winifred flashed in Marcus's mind and a red haze tinted his vision. A vampire barely mature enough to be allowed to wander alone was challenging him. He would tear the whelp limb from limb, burn his body in sunlight, and scatter the ashes. He channeled his blood through his palm and formed a fist that wrapped around Jonathan's neck, lifting him nearly to the ceiling. His brother clawed at the restraint and uttered a high-pitched sound that might have been a plea for mercy.

"Stay away from Winifred," Marcus said. "She is *mine*."

As quickly as it had started, the white-hot anger that burned in his chest faded. He released Jonathan to collapse into a heap and recalled his blood. Then he removed a handkerchief from his pocket and dabbed his damp forehead. He had not had such poor control over his emotions since he'd been a fledgling. It had to be another symptom of his affliction.

Jonathan struggled to his feet and gave Marcus a bewildered look. "What was that?"

Marcus swallowed the saliva that had accumulated in his mouth. He couldn't tell his brother the truth, that Cordon believed he was suffering from the same disease that had caused their maker to abandon them fifty years earlier. Jonathan had always been the closest to Marguerite and taken her disappearance and presumed death poorly. If Marcus revealed the extent of his illness, there was no telling how Jonathan would react. So rather than apologize or dismiss the incident as a mistake, Marcus squared his shoulders and tilted his head up, even though he could not look down his nose at his much-taller brother.

"A lesson," Marcus said coldly. "Our nest has become complacent." He tucked his hands behind his back. "I might have allowed Cordon to presume authority for the moment, but you would do well to remember that I am the eldest."

Jonathan straightened. "Y-Yes. Of course." Then he dropped to his knees and dipped his head. "I will obey your commands."

Chapter Eight

WINIFRED SAT IN front of a dressing table in her new room wearing the softest cotton night rail she owned and running a comb through her hair. Her attentive maids had already helped her bathe, plying her with a magical substance that had caused her usual wild curls to form soft ringlets, but she had to keep her hands busy to keep from peeling the loose skin at the edge of her thumb or absently plucking her eyebrows. It was far past the hour when she should have been asleep, but she couldn't stop thinking about Marcus.

They hadn't discussed how or when she would take up her duties as his assistant. In fact, the contrast between their energetic letters and the stilted conversation when he'd delivered her to her room couldn't have been starker.

She shook her head. This was ridiculous. He was her husband and she certainly would not be able to sleep until she clarified the bounds of their relationship and whether he'd agree to Felicity coming to live with them. Better to ask immediately rather than grow increasingly anxious by delaying.

With her mind made up, she donned a plush wool wrapper before venturing into the hallway. One of her maids had mentioned that Marcus spent his evenings in his workshop at the top of the north tower. With that in mind, she strode through her cavernous new home, her slippers slapping against the carpet runner and then bare stone. After several turns, she discovered a spiral staircase and climbed it until she'd found a wooden door braced with iron.

She knocked, but there was no response. Then she heard a loud slam, followed by a string of words that made her ears burn. Whatever Marcus was up to, he clearly needed her help. She tried knocking once more, and when there was no answer, she turned the knob and peered inside.

The circular room was stuffed with machines in various states of disassembly. A long, wooden desk filled with tools stood by a narrow window framed by thick, velvet curtains. She couldn't see Marcus, but she could hear him muttering, so she cracked the door open more until she spotted him crouching next to a large, cylindrical contraption. He wore black boots, brown trousers, and a loose, white shirt that gaped at the neck. He had one arm stuck to the elbow inside what she assumed was his latest invention, and the other was braced on the floor.

She licked her lips, aware that she was staring and should announce herself, but watching him work was fascinating. The awkward, quiet man who had led her to her room wasn't the Marcus she knew from her letters. Nor had she recognized the man who'd made halting conversation at her door before running away. But the figure in front of her, his cheeks red with exertion and his hair slick from hours of focus…*that* was the Marcus she knew. The tension that had been building in her from the moment he'd kissed her that afternoon vanished, replaced by a warmth that curled in her stomach and gave her the confidence she needed to step inside.

Marcus's head jerked in her direction. He withdrew his arm from the contraption and wiped his hands on his trousers. "Win—What, er, are you doing up so late?"

The concern in his large, brown eyes, the softness of his voice, and the triangle of pale skin showing through the top of his gaping shirt combined to chase every intelligent thought from her head. Instead of offering to help or asking him about Felicity or turning around and fleeing before she embarrassed herself further, all she did was stare.

He closed the space between them and put his hands gently on her shoulders. "Winifred. It is only me."

His use of her name jostled her senses back in order. She'd been an utter fool coming to him so late at night. He could have been furious at the invasion of his privacy. She had certainly snapped at her own cousin in the past when Felicity had barged into the library while Winifred had been deep in a tricky bit of translation.

"I apologize, my lord," she said. "I did not intend to interrupt."

"'My lord'?" He dropped his hands to her upper arms and squeezed. "When did I stop being 'Marcus'?"

"Marcus," she whispered. Then she breathed in sharply, taking in the smell of sweat and hot metal. Weeks of imagining their meeting, and not once had her mind supplied how he might have smelled. It was overwhelming, but she had not dared the freezing stairs to fall apart at the last moment. She swallowed past the lump in her throat and met his gaze. "Can I be of assistance?"

He scratched the base of his throat. "You want to help?"

"Yes." She would show him how useful she could be and hope that would sway his opinion when she brought up Felicity. She guessed that like any scientist, he could go hours without sleep or food while focused on a problem. As his assistant, she intended to provide him with anything he needed to continue working efficiently, even if that meant occasionally wrenching him out of his workshop to stretch his legs or take a walk in the sun.

His lips turned down. "It's been a long day. You should rest."

Now there was something she recognized, having heard similar statements from her cousin for years. She put her hands on her hips. "As should you. Nevertheless, we are both awake." She slid the sleeves of her wrapper up to her elbows. "Tell me what to do."

This was much better. Focusing on the task to be accomplished made it easier to not stare at his lips and remember how he'd pressed them to hers in such a light caress, or how his hands had felt on her shoulders. She'd come all the way across the ocean to be his assistant first and wife second.

"Well, if you insist," he said. "There is a loose bolt I can't reach. Hence…" He held up his grease-covered hands.

She giggled, then looked at her own palms and the slim, gold band he'd slipped onto her finger earlier. Wearing it while squeezing between heavy gears was a terrible idea. She'd read of working men who'd had entire parts of their body amputated because they'd failed to remove a bit of jewelry and it had become caught in machinery. She carefully slid the item off and was about to slip it into her pocket when Marcus said, "Wait."

He removed a chain from beneath his shirt, unclasped it, then held out one end. "It'll be more secure this way. You can tuck it beneath your clothes."

She stared at the necklace for several seconds before threading her wedding band onto it.

He held the chain so that the ring slid to the middle. "Turn around."

She did as he asked, then shivered as his arms came around her. A soft click indicated he'd done up the clasp. She lifted the necklace and placed it beneath her chemise so it nestled between her breasts atop the scar her uncle had given her years ago.

"Will that suffice?" he asked, his voice rougher than it had been a moment ago.

The hair on the back of her neck stood up. Rather than consider what the exchange meant, or wonder why the metal now lying against her bare skin wasn't warm from his body, she spun around. "Yes. Now, tell me what to do."

The skin around his eyes crinkled as he smiled. "Of course."

She followed him to the cylindrical machine he'd been working on as she'd entered, then waved at an opening. "You can access it here." He placed his hand on the smooth, metal exterior. "I can hear the bolt clicking when I turn the crankshaft."

She crouched until she was mere inches away from him, then slipped her hand inside.

Chapter Nine

MARCUS INHALED THE faintly soapy smell of Winifred's hair and kept his gaze firmly on her face instead of the smooth expanse of her neck, where arteries carrying her rich blood pulsed beneath the surface. The moment she'd stepped into his workshop, wide-eyed and wearing little more than a wrapper, he'd forgotten exactly why he'd fled her presence earlier.

She shifted her elbow. "I've got it, but it's caught."

He wrapped an arm around the base of his invention to keep it from toppling over. Nursing a broken bone would be a fine way to occupy her wedding night.

She twisted, inching closer. "Almost."

He should have moved away and supported the mechanism from the other side, but he was too fascinated by the warmth of her body and the wisps of her hair that caressed his skin. Faint, blue lines traced up her pale wrists and vanished beneath her sleeve. His mouth filled with saliva. A soft caress of her cheek and her resistance would vanish like sand flowing through his fingers. He could practically *taste* her hot blood trickling down his throat. She twisted her shoulder again and hit him square in the stomach with her elbow.

He winced but did not complain. For even considering biting her, he deserved it. No human had tempted him so in centuries.

"I think I have it," she said.

Of course she had accomplished what he'd been failing at for weeks. They had only been married a few hours, and she'd already proven her worth.

She started to remove her hand from inside his invention but only made it a few inches before she stopped. "My hand is wedged."

"Release the bolt."

"I did," she said. "But I still can't…" She squirmed around. "I'm… I'm stuck."

Her rapidly increasing pulse riled his instincts and made his jaw ache with the effort of holding back his fangs.

"Look at me," he said.

She stopped struggling and met his gaze.

"I'm going to help you," he said. "To do that, I need to touch you in a manner that might make you uncomfortable. You must remain still, no matter what happens. Do you understand?"

Her cheeks reddened. "Yes."

He positioned his long limbs until her head was nestled against his chest. Then he maneuvered his arm inside the mechanism beneath hers. After he freed her, he would take a sledgehammer to the damned thing, but for now, he had to hope his powers would not fail him. He tucked his arm more securely about her back, then forced his blood into his arm and through his pores until it pooled around his fingertips.

"What are you doing?" Winifred asked.

"Giving you more room," he lied.

He willed his blood around her bruised flesh, then formed it into a solid mass that expanded until the pressure made the gears groan.

"Try now," he said between gritted teeth.

She jerked her arm out in one smooth movement.

He released his hold on the blood and fell onto his rear, nearly taking his wretched invention with him.

"Marcus!" She grasped his upper arms. "Are you hurt?"

He tucked his battered limb behind his back for the few seconds it took for his wounds to heal. When his skin no longer itched, he pushed to his feet. She remained close, her outstretched hands hovering a few inches from his chest, as if she expected him to collapse. He used the opportunity to examine her arm, which was streaked with grease but appeared otherwise whole.

"I apologize," he said. "I would not have allowed you to help if I'd thought you might injure yourself." He turned to his invention and kicked it. The pile of steel and iron tottered back and forth on its wide base but did not fall. "This thing has given me no end of grief."

Winifred gave him one last penetrating glance, as if telling him she disapproved of his treatment of his creation, but then she ran her fingers over the smooth block of mahogany that topped the machine. "What's inside?"

"Samples of blood from my livestock." He grasped the handle and turned it. Gears groaned, and there was a clicking within from the bolt they had failed to retrieve, but the wooden block spun. "I'm attempting to identify the toxin in their blood, but I've yet to find a speed that will produce a clean separation." His attempts had thus far resulted in several boxes of shattered glass. Metal vials would have solved that problem, but then he lost the ability to discern the layers in his concoctions visually without first somehow transferring the liquid to a different receptacle. He'd commissioned thicker glass containers from an artisan in the village, but they had not yet been delivered.

Winifred brought her hand to her mouth, covering her yawn. Behind her, the sky through the window was painted in shades of red. He had perhaps an hour before he would have to rest, which meant she had been awake half the night. "You require sleep."

She tugged her sleeves down. "I suppose you are right." She lifted the chain from beneath her wrapper, opened the latch, removed her ring, then placed the necklace in her palm and held it out. "Thank you for letting me borrow this."

He was tempted to tell her to keep it. He had hundreds of others. But he wanted the first gift he gave her to be something more meaningful. An item she would never forget. So, he returned the chain to his neck and slipped it beneath his shirt so the metal, warm from being in contact with her breast, sat flush against his skin.

"I must admit," she said as they made their way to the door. "This is not at all what I imagined for my wedding night."

His heart clenched. They had been married for less than a day and he'd already disappointed her.

She tilted her chin up and smiled. "It's much better."

He sagged with relief. "I am glad."

A heavy silence settled between them, broken only by the soft patter of rain on the window. He should have agreed with her assessment, or offered to escort her to her room, or at least wished her pleasant dreams, but the words stuck in his throat.

Her smile faltered. Without saying a word, she turned around, placed her hand on the knob, then flinched.

He closed his fingers around her wrist. "What is it? Are you injured?"

"It is nothing."

He gently lifted her hand and turned it over so her palm faced up, revealing a long cut along the side of her thumb. A crimson bead formed on the wound. Before he could consider the wisdom of his actions, he ducked his head, took her digit into his mouth, and rasped the flat of his tongue over the injury. She tasted like sunlight and freedom, fresh and bright. More than anything, he wanted to sink his teeth into the thick artery running down her wrist. His fangs descended. He ran their sharp points over her skin but did not pierce.

She moaned.

He'd taken things too far. She was his assistant, not a pleasant diversion. It had been centuries since he'd drunk from a human, and all it had taken to break his vow was a single abrasion. It was shameful and would never happen again. He retracted his fangs and straightened. "I apologize. I should not have touched you without your permission."

"I did not dislike it," she said.

He swallowed thickly. "Pardon?"

She licked her lips. "Just now. I enjoyed what… you did." Her cheeks were red, and her spectacles were fogging. "In fact, I was hoping you would touch me. So, you did not have to apologize. I, ah, will leave you to your work." Then she gathered her skirts and raced down the steps.

He stared after her until she turned a corner. He could not have heard her right. Was it possible she was interested in pursuing physical intimacy? There was nothing stopping them. Even if they hadn't been living together in a castle, far away from his judgmental peers, they were married. Her own mother probably assumed they'd already consummated their union.

A sudden image of Winifred sprawled on his bed dressed in a sheer nightgown entered his mind, causing him to flush. It had been nearly a decade since he'd bedded a woman, human or otherwise.

When he was sure she'd returned to her room, he rushed down the steps and back to his bedchamber. The curtains were already drawn and a fire lit in the hearth. He picked up the goblet sitting beside the fire and drained it. After the banquet that had been Winifred's blood, drinking the substance was like consuming what was left in a mop bucket after cleaning the floors. He set the empty glass aside, wiped his mouth, and recalled the thrum of heat that had shot through him when he'd tasted her.

Having her nearby soothed the chasm in his heart that had deepened with every year he'd remained separated from his nest siblings. It was not something he would ever speak aloud, but until Winifred had arrived, he'd been desperately lonely. Maintaining a detached indifference became more difficult with each passing day.

He fell onto his bed, freed his throbbing cock from his trousers, and stroked himself. Everything about Winifred was intoxicating. The faint scent of strawberries in her breath, the soft curves of her shoulders, the way she'd leaned into his touch and run the tip of her tongue along her bottom lip. She'd nearly come apart from the slight touch of his fang.

As the orgasm ripped through his body, he curled onto his side, wrapped his arms around a pillow, and imagined it was his wife.

Chapter Ten

WHEN WINIFRED AWOKE at sunrise, it was with a sense of bubbling excitement she hadn't experienced in years, despite the absurdly early hour. If she closed her eyes, she could almost feel Marcus's icy, chapped lips pressed to her palm and his tongue caressing her thumb. It had been far more intimate than the chaste kiss they'd shared, and she found she was almost as eager to see him again as she was to find the expansive library he'd described in his letters.

Before any of that, however, she had to properly meet the staff. Her new role as the mistress of the household came with responsibilities.

A knock had her drawing back the covers. "Come in."

A slight girl bustled inside, wearing a white, frilly apron over a light-blue blouse, a skirt of a slightly darker color, and a white bonnet covering her coal-black hair. It was the same maid who had assisted Winifred with donning and removing her wedding dress the previous evening. The girl dipped into a deep curtsey. "Good morning, my lady."

Winifred blinked. She's nearly forgotten her new title. It would be difficult to get used to being referred to in such a manner. She was tempted to tell the maid to call her by her given name, but she knew enough about the social hierarchy of a proper household to dismiss the idea. It would only strain her relationship with the staff, who would most likely prefer formality.

Not to mention, if Winifred's mother heard any of the servants speaking so casually to their new employer, Mrs. Belltree would undoubtedly express her disapproval by making herself even more of a nuisance than usual.

The young maid rose from her curtsey. "I am Flora Keenan."

"Keenan," Winifred repeated.

The maid turned to the wardrobe. "What would you like to wear today, my lady?"

"The indigo print cotton day dress with the cap sleeves," she said. It was fine enough for her tour of the castle, but not so tight-fitting that she would be uncomfortable. After her family departed, she would endeavor to find out how to purchase new garments, but for now, the clothing she had transported from Toronto would suffice.

When Keenan had dressed her and tamed her wild hair by braiding it into a lovely plait, Winifred felt ready to take up her responsibilities. It would be a long day, but her mother had seen to it she'd achieved a proper education that had included everything the wife of a lord had to know.

Even if she'd rather have spent the day reading.

Hours later, as she bit into her third cucumber sandwich from inside the glass-enclosed solarium she'd discovered on the second floor, she cursed her poor choice of slippers. The halls were almost entirely without carpeting or rugs, which meant that much less padding between the sensitive soles of her feet and the hard stone. She would have to invest in better footwear as soon as possible.

The morning had been a flurry of activity. Mrs. Gillanders had insisted upon leading her through the entire building, even having the staff line up along the wall. There weren't nearly as many servants as she'd expected, perhaps because Marcus was not known for entertaining. She was now the employer of nearly fifty people, most of whom lived in the village. That was a surprise, as the castle was more than large enough to house twice as many. When she'd asked Mrs. Gillanders, the woman had blushed and muttered something about ghosts that had made Winifred chuckle. After that, Winifred had approved menus and selected activities to entertain her guests for the afternoon. The scope of it all was exhausting, but it was a small price to pay. In a few days, her guests would leave, and then she would be free.

Assuming Marcus kept his promises.

"Did you have a restful night?" Felicity asked as she dipped a biscuit into her tea. She had joined Winifred during her tour of the castle. Mrs. Gillanders had huffed at the addition, but Winifred hadn't had the heart to send her cousin away.

"I assisted Marcus in his workshop," Winifred said.

Felicity's grin fell. "You spent your first night as a married woman engaged in a *scientific inquiry?*" She chuckled. "I should not be surprised. Perhaps I was wrong when I counseled you against this marriage. It does seem to suit you."

"I would hope so. That is why I came all the way across the ocean, after all. If all I'd wanted was a suitable marriage, I could have chosen from the many eligible gentlemen in Toronto." What Marcus offered was invaluable; an opportunity to be closer to her cousin and pursue her research to her heart's content. Most men would have insisted she occupy her time with more ladylike pursuits. Felicity's brother, Vincent, for example, had once bribed a maid into helping him steal books from Winifred's bedchamber after she'd slighted him in public. She couldn't imagine Marcus ever behaving so pettily.

"Did you ask him about hiring me?" Felicity asked.

Winifred shook her head. "The moment did not feel right. I am waiting for the perfect opportunity to increase the chances of success."

She picked up a garlic and cheese scone. They were buttery and soft without being too crumbly. She ate two before a servant arrived with a glass dish containing something called Cranachan. At the first bite, she closed her eyes and sighed. The combination of oats, honey, and fresh raspberries was delightful.

Felicity spun her saucer in circles with her fingertips. "I cannot stop thinking that this entire situation is unusual. Have you noticed there are hardly any mirrors, and every window has thick drapes? It makes me wonder what the earl is trying to hide."

Winifred sipped her drink to keep from responding with a sharp retort. First Felicity had cautioned her against marrying Marcus, then she'd had suggested Winifred's new husband was dangerous, and now this? It was difficult not to feel insulted on Marcus's behalf. "He simply prefers solitude."

"Perhaps," Felicity said. "But then why ask you to come all this way?"

Winifred tamped down her irritation. "What do you mean?"

Felicity heaved a sigh. "Why find a wife in Canada when there are plenty of ladies in Scotland who would have leaped at a chance to become a countess? There must be something else the earl wants from you."

"An assistant," Winifred said quickly, but her words lacked the conviction she'd intended. A small part of her shared Felicity's concern. Marcus was wealthy, handsome, and titled. The daughter of newly wealthy merchants was hardly an excellent match in comparison.

"I envy you," Felicity blurted out.

Winifred almost choked. Her daring cousin, a woman who refused to back down from any challenge, no matter how foolish…envied her. The bookish wallflower who spent so much time lost in books that there was a chaise in her parents' library permanently impressioned with the shape of her body. It was so ridiculous, it made her burst into laughter.

"It's true," Felicity said. She furrowed her brow and stared into her empty cup. "You knew exactly what you wanted and when an opportunity presented itself, you seized it." Her shoulders slumped. "Meanwhile, our uncle will not even grant me an audience to discuss my future, and Vincent spends several nights a month working on a secret project in the basement."

Vincent working on a secret project? Winifred thought that unlikely. The man had never expressed an interested in science or crafts.

Felicity pursed her lips. "Lately, I feel like an intruder in my own home."

Winifred reached across the table and put her hand on top of her cousin's. "I'm sorry. You have my word that I will speak to the earl about it today."

Felicity shook her head. "Enough about me. Tell me more about him."

Winifred sighed. She did not like Felicity's evasiveness, but she knew her cousin well enough to not steer the conversation back to an obviously painful topic. She would have to come up with a different way to find out what was bothering Felicity.

"He is an inventor, as you know," Winifred said. "His workshop is full of the most remarkable machines." Including the one she had assisted him with that used centrifugal force. Seeing his experiments made her feel strangely at ease with her unusual situation. It would have been easy for him to lie in his letters, to pretend to be something he wasn't, but everything she'd seen since arriving suggested Marcus was exactly as she'd expected: an intelligent but desperately lonely man. His need for assistance was not because of any lack of skill or knowledge, but the inevitable result of working alone for an extended length of time. He'd become trapped in his own mind and lost the perspective that was necessary for true innovation.

"What is his topic of interest?" Felicity asked.

"I am not entirely sure." Despite having corresponded for months, she knew vanishingly little about what he was trying to achieve. He had mentioned an illness in his livestock, but he had not specified what he would do when he identified the cause.

"Wait," Felicity said. She checked the time on her delicate rose gold chatelaine watch. "We have nearly an hour until your mother is likely to awaken. Why are we lounging about drinking tea when we could be exploring the library?"

Winifred laughed. "I suppose you are right."

They had uttered identical gasps when Mrs. Gillanders had swung open the doors during the tour, but the housekeeper had barely given them a minute to admire the impressive space before she'd moved on.

Felicity rose. "Shall we?"

"Yes," Winifred said. "We shall."

The two women exited the solarium, arm-in-arm. When they arrived at their destination, Winifred barely suppressed a squeal. Marcus had not been exaggerating when he'd described his library. It must have been a ballroom at one point, as the floor was polished marble, but there were rows upon rows of shelves, as far as she could see. Winifred met Felicity's gaze, and in that moment, an understanding passed between them. They enjoyed each other's company, but a treasure such as the one before them required solitary investigation.

Felicity turned left, and Winifred right.

To Winifred's immense satisfaction, the first books she ran her fingers over were historical manuscripts. Most she had read, but there were a few she did not recognize. She removed several and tucked them beneath her arm before continuing to the next shelf. It was less exciting, containing dusty religious tomes and treatises on various sciences. She had more luck several minutes later as she stumbled on truly rare handwritten journals of explorers. She had to restrain herself from heaping them all in her arms—there were only so many she could read in a day—but she made a mental note to ask Marcus where he had found them.

As she turned toward the window, a set of bright-blue spines caught her attention. She tugged one out and flipped it open to a random page, which contained a remarkably detailed illustration of a naked couple.

Her cheeks warmed. Was it even possible to contort one's body in such a manner? It seemed as if it would be quite painful, although the woman on the page certainly did not appear to be in distress. Her eyes were closed, but her expression was one of bliss.

Winifred leaned against a bookshelf and imagined Marcus sliding his palms up her shins and pressing ardent kisses to her stomach. The secret place between her thighs throbbed, making her wish for the privacy of her room.

Unfortunately, her time was not yet her own.

She reluctantly closed the book and added it to the top of her teetering stack. Perhaps she was torturing herself by keeping it, but the way Marcus had touched her the previous night had sparked an unexpected interest in pursuing the physical aspects of marriage. If nothing else, the illustrations would be something titillating to look at when she lay in her bed alone at night.

Heavily laden with texts, she made her way to a table by a window and settled in a stiff-backed wooden chair. She opened the first of her books, tilted the pages into the sunlight, and immersed herself in a different world.

Chapter Eleven

MARCUS RAN HIS fingers over the grain of the oak door at the bottom of his tower. Such a simple thing, a chunk of wood and iron lashed together to serve the noble purpose of keeping unwanted intruders out.

It wasn't doing a very good job.

Not only was his castle filled with strangers, but now he couldn't so much as *think* about venturing outside without being overwhelmed with a suffocating sense of pressure, like all the air had been sucked out of his lungs. He assumed the worsening of his symptoms was because of the disruption in his carefully crafted routine, but he couldn't help wondering if Cordon was right and hunters were responsible.

He was about to try again, asphyxiation be damned, when he heard the rapid sound of footfalls descending the steps.

"There you are," Cordon said as he came around the corner. There was loose hay stuck to his trousers, the knot of his cravat was askew, and a button on his silver-and-blue-striped jacket was missing.

"You look like you had a fight with a horse and lost," Marcus said before Cordon could ask questions Marcus didn't want to answer. Being rescued by his brother once had been embarrassing enough. He could think of nothing worse than Cordon discovering the depths of his vulnerability. The man could not keep anything to himself. The next thing Marcus knew, his siblings would be stolen away by other nests desperate to supplement their numbers while he remained trapped in his stone prison.

Better to continue his experiments in secret.

Cordon flicked a clump of dirt off his shoulder. "I had an unfortunate encounter with a spooked stallion. The creature escaped from its pen and was making a glutton of itself, eating a heap of turnips someone had dumped in the pasture. You should have them removed before your cows get to them." He glanced down at himself and grimaced. "Kitty will be furious when she sees the mess I've made."

That was likely true. Katherine "Kitty" Shaw, Cordon's new wife, had been a dressmaker and tailor before Cordon had turned her into a vampire. Not attending their wedding with the rest of his nest was one of Marcus's biggest regrets. But Marguerite would not have allowed sentimentality to sway her mood, so he couldn't, either.

Even if his three sisters' absence at his own wedding had hurt more than he cared to admit.

"Why were you in a stable?" Marcus asked.

Cordon swiped more hay from the fabric of his clothing with his hands. "Returning from doing as you asked. I investigated Lucina's reports."

"What did you discover?"

Cordon untied his cravat and looped it around his neck. "Nothing good. The murdered vampires in Glasgow were ravaged by some kind of animal, beheaded, and left in places where the sun would not reach them."

Marcus sucked his teeth. Now he understood why Lucina had sent Cordon to warn him. If the vampires had been killed by a member of their own kind, there would have been no bodies left behind. Only a hunter would take the precaution of severing their victims' heads and keeping them away from sunlight so they wouldn't turn to ash.

Someone was sending a message.

"I have worse news," Jonathan said, appearing behind Cordon as if by magic. Jonathan could do that; move about without being noticed by anyone, human or vampire. It was a skill he used to liberate priceless vampiric artifacts from private collections around the world.

"I wish you wouldn't do that," Cordon said with a frown.

"What did you discover?" Marcus asked.

Jonathan put an arm around Cordon's shoulders. "A symbol of a sun in a circle carved on the side of the local tavern."

"A sun," Marcus repeated. There was something strangely familiar about that description.

Cordon stepped away from Jonathan. "What were you doing in the village?"

Jonathan put a hand over his heart. "Following orders, of course."

"You were supposed to be watching Miss Belltree's family."

"You mean Lady Kingsbury's family," Jonathan said wryly.

Marcus inhaled sharply. His brother was right. Winifred was no longer a mere figure in his dreams. She was his *wife*. A pleasant warmth bloomed in his chest.

Cordon was still staring at their youngest brother.

Jonathan threw up his arms. "Fine! I took a well-deserved break."

Cordon scowled. "As always, our brother has a questionable relationship with the truth."

Jonathan's eyes gleamed blue. "At least I have not gone soft."

"What does that mean?"

Marcus held up his hand. "That is enough."

Both men stood down, to Marcus's relief. They tested his patience but remained obedient. He did not yet have to worry about one of them challenging his leadership.

"What are your orders?" Cordon asked.

Marcus exhaled slowly. "Jonathan, continue to watch the guests and report unusual activity. Cordon, get Helena to search the archives. See if you can track down any hunter families that might be associated with the sun symbol."

He knew he'd seen it before but couldn't remember where.

Jonathan put a hand on his hip. "What are you going to do?"

Marcus cracked his stiff shoulders. "I'm going to question my wife."

MARCUS FOUND WINIFRED asleep in the library with her cousin Miss Sorrow lounging on a nearby window ledge. When the black-haired young lady noticed him, she flattened the book she'd been reading to her chest and scrunched her nose. "Kingsbury."

He ignored her rudeness and inclined his head. "Good evening, Miss Sorrow. Has my collection met with your approval?"

She hopped from her perch. "The *library* is magnificent. I have yet to decide how I feel about the man who assembled it." She glanced at Winifred, and her face softened. "She is the only true friend I've ever had."

She was protective of her cousin. He was familiar with the feeling. Before his confinement, he had been endlessly frustrated by his younger sibling's reckless behavior. On more than one occasion, he'd dragged his youngest brother out of a gambling hell minutes before sunrise because Jonathan had "lost track of time."

Felicity sighed. "Oh, Winnie. You really can sleep through anything."

Winifred had her head on her folded arms and let out an occasional snore.

"Take care of her, my lord," Felicity said. "She's more sensitive than she seems." Then she spun around and strode out of the room.

He returned his attention to his slumbering wife. He didn't want to believe she could have anything to do with the hunters, but the safety of his nest had to come first. Therefore, he let her rest while he made a few choice selections from his shelves. The best way to earn her trust was to give her what she'd crossed the ocean for.

When he dropped the books on the desk, she jerked upright.

"Hello," he said. "Have you been enjoying my collection?"

She covered her mouth as she yawned, then grinned. "It is exceptional."

He gestured to the table. "I thought these might interest you."

She flipped open the first book as he watched over her shoulder. The text was ancient, the pages so yellow, they almost appeared dyed and moved with a crackling stiffness.

"My, ah, grandfather's journals," he said, crafting the lie as he spoke. "He was present at the eruption of Mount Tambora and wrote of the experience."

They were, of course, *his* journals, but he couldn't reveal that yet. For the moment, it was best to continue to masquerade as a human.

"Thank you," she said with a wide smile. "I could not ask for a better gift."

He slid into the chair across from her. She certainly didn't seem anxious, but that didn't prove anything. His enemy was adept at infiltration. Before the Wild Hunt had all but eradicated them, he'd once spent three weeks following a group of suspected hunters, only to discover they had been secretly watching him the entire time. "I am glad you approve."

She ran her hands over the spines. "Did you require my assistance with your invention?"

A genuine desire to be helpful, or a ploy to get him alone again? Regardless, he couldn't allow her access to his workshop until he discovered her intentions. There were notebooks and artifacts stored inside that hunters would find extraordinarily valuable.

"There is no need. I disposed of it."

It wasn't as if he'd made much progress. Twenty-eight concoctions and none of them had provided lasting relief. He'd even collected his own blood and compared it against samples reluctantly extracted from his siblings but had discovered nothing that would explain why he suffered attacks and the others did not.

There was always Cordon's theory that everything Marcus was experiencing was part of mate atrophy, but Cordon's illness several months prior had included entirely different symptoms. In any case, Marcus couldn't leave the castle, and he wasn't about to begin summoning young women to join him until he found his mate.

No, he would continue his search for an alternative solution.

Winifred tilted her head. "How am I to assist you, then?"

He ran his tongue over his teeth. There was no trace of malice or guile in her tone, but Cordon was right that he knew very little about her. "Do not worry about that for now."

"In that case," she said. "Perhaps I could ask a favor."

His shoulders tensed. "You may ask."

She rubbed her hands together. "It is my cousin Felicity. She would be an excellent addition to our household. As my companion."

"You want to hire your cousin?" He almost laughed. It was such a simple request. "If that is what you wish, you have my permission." The cost was nothing to him, and having another woman around might make it easier for Winifred to live so far from society.

Her eyes shone, and when she spoke, her voice was hoarse. "Thank you, Marcus. Oh, thank you! You do not know how much this means to me."

Her display of emotion made his heart leap into his throat. He had grown so used to his siblings treating him with apathy or hostility that being on the receiving end of such gratitude left him unsure of how to react. What he wanted to do was lift her in his arms and bury his nose in her hair. Instead, he tapped the stack of books. "May I read to you?"

She had written about how her cousin had often done the same in Toronto. By repeating that positive experience, she might become more comfortable in his presence and inadvertently reveal secrets.

As expected, she brightened. "Would you?"

"Of course."

He opened his journal and smoothed his hand over a page. "'The storm appeared as if by magic, settling over the bay with such fearsome speed that half my crewmates were asleep when the sky was clear and awoke to being jostled out of their bunks.'"

She rose and slid into the seat next to him. "When was this?"

He flipped back. "1775, on the coast of Newfoundland. The storm would now be classified as a hurricane."

She opened a notebook and began scribbling, which he took as a sign to continue. But when he looked at the next page, the print was smudged and unreadable. He mentally brought himself back to that night and pretended to continue reading.

"I struggled to the deck, where a dozen figures were flitting around, shouting even though their voices were lost to the fury of the wind. They tied ropes around their waists and attached themselves to the ship, but that proved a fatal idea." He remembered the flash of yellow slicker coats running around the deck of the ship to which he'd been posted. "The rain struck like thousands of sharp stones, and the wind thrashed the sails back and forth. I joined two other men trying to rein them in, but the storm was too strong. George was the first to be swept away, the rope around his waist becoming loose enough that when a wave washed over the deck, he was thrown ten feet in the air and landed on a broken railing. I will never forget the bloodied wood sticking out of his chest and the way he screamed as he pawed impotently at the protrusion, as if he could bat it away."

"It sounds awful," she said. She'd sidled so close, he could hear the rapid thrum of her pulse.

He tried not to smile at the excitement in her voice and resisted the urge to drape his arm around her shoulders. "The sky was almost perfectly clear, like an enormous hand had scooped up all the clouds as far as I could see and whipped them into a single, fearsome funnel. Lightning sparked along the edges of the hurricane as if holding it in the sky."

The sound of her pencil sliding along the paper made him look up. She was sketching as he described.

"That's not quite right," he said as she created a thin body for the hurricane.

She stilled and tilted her drawing so he could see it. "Do you think it was taller?"

"No." He reached for her notebook before stopping himself. "May I?"

She slid it across the table. He picked up her pencil and tilted it so it formed a softer mark. "It was—would have been—more like a wine cork, quite bulbous." He used the edge of his hand to smear the marks. "The exact boundary would have been difficult to define, as it shifted and warped, always turning and reforming. I—ah, *my grandfather* describes it in more detail on a later page." He drew a tiny person standing on the grass to show the size of the cloud.

She touched the figure. "Is that him?"

He chuckled. "No." He curved a line between the figure and the cloud, then drew wavy lines. "The sea." He sketched the rough shape of a long ship with three masts. "The ship. It sank that day, taking most of the crew with it, including my grandfather." He realized too late the flaw in his story, that his 'grandfather's' death would not explain the existence of the journals, and quickly added, "He survived, of course. By clinging to flotsam for hours in the freezing water until rescue arrived."

"This is remarkable," she said. "It's almost as if you were actually *there*."

He shuddered. The scene on the paper was exactly like he remembered. He could almost hear the howl of the wind and feel the sheeting rain striking his face. It was not a memory he wished to keep. He should have been goading her to discuss her family but was delving into his own past instead. If she was a hunter, she was damned good at subversion.

She flipped her notebook closed. "I wish I could see it myself. Reading about what happened is marvelous, but actually visiting the ruins of an ancient city, or climbing up a volcano..." She trailed off, then gently placed her hand on top of his. "Perhaps we could go together?"

He gulped. She had the look of a woman intent on getting what she wanted. Over his long existence, he'd been in similar situations hundreds of times, but not once had he felt so uncertain. Further intimacy between them was a terrible idea, given his weakened condition and suspicions about her. He didn't possess the control to have her so close without giving into the urge to drink from her again.

"What I said last night..." she said as her cheeks turned red. "I was being truthful. I enjoyed what we...what you did."

His fangs throbbed at the memory of her blood sliding down his throat. He wanted to taste her. Not just the inside of her mouth, but her breasts, her thighs, and the sweetness of her quim. More than anything, he ached to plunge his fangs into her flesh at the same time he brought her to orgasm so that her pleasure would thrum through them and make their joining that much more intense.

He jerked his hand out from under hers. His lustful thoughts meant he was not in control. He had to put distance between them, and he knew exactly how to dampen her desire.

By telling her the truth.

"Winifred, there is something you must know."

She tilted her head. "Oh?"

He cleared his throat. "I appreciate your interest, but I could not join you on excursions to historical sites because I cannot leave this castle."

"You can't..." Winifred gave him a small smile that didn't quite reach her eyes. "I understand that you have lived as a recluse. It is not my intention to force you to attend social events."

"It is not that," he said. "I have not left the grounds in nearly a decade."

Winifred was silent for a full minute before she burst into

high-pitched laughter.

The cheek of the wretched woman. He would tackle her to the ground, pin her in place, and bare his fangs until she submitted. Then he'd drag her back to his bedchamber and use his many talents to make her scream his name until her voice became hoarse.

No.

He was more than his nature. It would not rule him.

"O-Oh, Marcus," she said between gasps. "I did not expect you to have such a dry wit." She dabbed her cheeks with a handkerchief. "An earl confined to his castle who summons a wife from across the ocean. It is like the beginning of a story."

"I am glad you find my situation so humorous."

She dropped her handkerchief. It fluttered to the table. "You are serious." Her face paled until her skin was nearly the color of her handkerchief. "Is it some manner of punishment? Are you a criminal?"

He straightened. "No!"

"Then what keeps you here? Do you suffer from an ailment?" Her brows drew together in sympathy. "Consumption?"

She was a threat. A challenge to his authority. He could not let her live. One bite and she'd be at his mercy. He shoved to his feet so quickly that his chair toppled over sideways. "Enough questions."

She straightened, and it was like an entirely different woman was standing in front of him, one who was as expressionless as a statue. She squeezed her books to her chest. "What do you want from me, Marcus? Why am I here?"

His mouth went dry. Any answer he could give would be a lie or would reveal truths about himself that he did not yet want her to know. An icy numbness crept up his legs and his vision darkened at the edges.

"I-I required an assistant," he said. "That is all." Then he turned around and did what he did best.

He ran away.

Chapter Twelve

WINIFRED FLED THE library in a rush, not caring that the slap of her slippers echoed through the hall. It had taken less than a day for Marcus to reveal his true nature. Felicity had been right all along. She dashed tears from her eyes. Becoming upset would accomplish nothing. Regardless of any emotional pain, her situation was still a tremendous improvement over Toronto. Here, she had a position of privilege, a title, and plenty of time to study the wealth of books at her disposal. Not to mention, he had consented to her request for a companion.

She slowed her pace. That was right; she would still have Felicity. She could suppress her unwanted attraction to Marcus and even continue to act as his assistant if it meant saving Felicity from their uncle.

With her mood significantly improved, she turned the corner and spotted her mother standing outside her room. For a moment, she considered turning around and returning to the library, but then Mrs. Belltree met her gaze and Winifred knew any chance she had of spending the rest of the day reading had vanished.

"There you are," her mother said with a scowl. "I have been looking for you for hours."

Winifred clasped her hands at her waist. "Good morning, Mother."

Mrs. Belltree tutted. "Did you learn nothing from your governess?" She gestured at Winifred's floral patterned cotton day dress. "You have *guests*, my dear." She sighed. "Your uncle has arrived and wishes to speak to you."

Winifred squeezed her hands together so tightly that her fingertips prickled. Her uncle had come to retrieve Felicity. That was the only reasonable explanation for why he would have traveled such a distance when he had not attended the wedding. He couldn't know Winifred was about to wrest his niece from his clutches. "Perhaps I should change—"

Her mother shook her head. "You have dawdled long enough." She linked her arm with Winifred's and drew her down the hall.

"Do not fret. I am certain he only intends to offer congratulations."

That was unlikely. Ethan Sorrow was about as sentimental as an ancient teacher at the school Winifred had attended in Toronto. Lady Joy, as the pupils had ironically called her, had been prone to swatting the heads of her students with a long ruler whenever they'd answered a question wrong.

At least Winifred did not have to worry about receiving similar treatment from her uncle.

She hoped.

Her mother led her down the stairs to the drawing room, where three people were waiting. The first was Felicity, who was wearing the brown twill dress she hated, along with black kidskin gloves and leather boots. It was an outfit she reserved for traveling. She kept her gaze firmly on her lap as Winifred entered, likely because Vincent lounged on the settee beside her with an arm thrown over the back. There were clumps of dirt stuck to the soles of his boots and flecks of the same on the carpet at his feet.

The last person in the room was the three cousins' uncle, Mr. Ethan Sorrow. He was dressed in a black-on-black suit, as if he'd just returned from a funeral, and his thin, silver-gray hair was slicked back over his skull. He sat stiff-backed on a plush parlor chair and acknowledged Winifred's entry into the room with a slight incline of his head.

"Thank you, Margaret," Uncle Ethan said, addressing Winifred's mother. "It has been too long." He leaned forward. "It is such a shame you moved so far out of reach."

"Ethan," Mrs. Belltree said, her voice cold. "Do you intend to stay long?"

He scoffed. "Pleasant as always, sister. I am so very glad we've kept on good terms. In answer to your question, no. I have no desire to sleep beneath the same roof as a turncoat."

Then he waved his hand in clear dismissal.

Mrs. Belltree shot a worried glance at Winifred before dipping into a curtsey and leaving her daughter poised in front of her family, feeling as if she were perched on the edge of a cliff, staring down at the frothy ocean washing over sharp rocks.

"Do not stand there like a child waiting to be chastised," Uncle Ethan said. "Sit."

She winced but did as he'd bidden by taking the chair opposite him. She spared another glance at Felicity, but her cousin's attention remained fixed on her lap. That meant the topic of this conversation was likely not going to be pleasant.

Uncle Ethan snapped his fingers. The doors creaked open, and three maids bustled inside without a word, placing a tea set and a plate of fragrant-smelling scones on the table between Winifred and her uncle. It happened with such speed that Winifred suspected they'd been waiting at the door.

She reached for the teapot and poured four cups, then handed three to her guests. When Vincent accepted his, his nostrils flared, and he gave her a nasty grin. Before she could remark on it, Felicity whispered a barely audible, "Don't."

Winifred was not one to ignore a warning from her cousin. She plastered a pleasant smile on her face and looked at her uncle. "Did you come to offer well wishes?"

He picked up a scone. "Your union to the earl was a mistake."

She hurriedly set down her cup before she spilled. "P-Pardon?"

He took a large bite and chewed slowly. All the while, Winifred felt ready to leap out of her chair. First, he had ordered her servants about as if he was the owner of the house, and now he insulted her marriage. The only thing that kept her silent was Felicity's whispered warning.

"Your father should have contacted me before arranging the match," Uncle Ethan said. "As he did not, I must assume my sister, your mother, has neglected her responsibilities." He picked up his teacup. "Tell me what you know of our ancestors."

Winifred brought her hand to her breast, where the family crest was burned into her skin. "My grandfather, Bernard Sorrow, was married to—"

Uncle Ethan sliced his hand through the air. "Not your pedigree. Their mission."

A shiver went down Winifred's spine. He could only be referring to the tales that had amused her as a girl until her uncle had convinced his siblings to force a pair of knobby-kneed girls to undergo an ancient rite of initiation that had left them both physically and mentally scarred. After that traumatic night, Winifred had vowed to put their families' absurd history behind her. But she remembered enough from her early lessons to answer.

"T-They were hunters," she said. "They tracked down individuals who were suspected to be—"

"Monsters," Vincent said, spitting the word as if it were a curse. "They hunted and killed monsters. And you *married* one."

Winifred's jaw dropped open. She hurriedly closed it. They could not possibly be referring to Marcus. Despite his recent show of temper, he'd shown her only kindness.

"I see your ignorance regarding your ancestors is worse than I thought," Uncle Ethan said. "Excuse your cousin. What he means is that our family has been in a… feud with the Devilles for several years." He sighed. "Now you have joined them. This puts me in a difficult position."

She squeezed her hands in her lap. "What do you mean? What feud?"

Uncle Ethan picked up a second scone and bit into it. Winifred did not dare move or speak. Even Felicity was as pale as a sheet.

At last, Uncle Ethan swallowed. Then he brushed crumbs from his lap, picked up his gold-handled cane from the floor, and stood. "With your union to the earl, you have allied yourself with his family instead of your own. Therefore, your name has been erased from our family ledger." His expression softened. "I am sorry. There was no other choice. As for you"—he looked at Felicity—"it is best you remember that until you come of age, you are my responsibility. You are forbidden from associating from Winifred." He glanced at Vincent. "Both of you."

Vincent scowled but did not refute the statement.

"No," Winifred whispered as she took in her cousin's trembling shoulders. Even if Felicity ran away from Uncle Ethan's home, he had the right to drag her back until she turned one-and-twenty. Winifred had agreed to marry Marcus to escape from her parents and achieve the independence she craved, but it had also been with the understanding she could save Felicity from their uncle. She hadn't even told her cousin that Marcus had agreed to let her live with them. Now she couldn't even *write* to her cousin. It was beyond cruel.

She stood. "Please, Uncle—"

"That is enough," Uncle Ethan said, speaking over her. Then he rose and quickly left the room, with Felicity following behind. The only person who remained was Vincent.

"This is not over," he whispered. "You are mine. I won't give up so easily."

With that ominous warning, he exited, leaving Winifred to hold back her tears and curse herself for not fighting harder. She wasn't a young girl anymore; she was a countess. Uncle Ethan shouldn't have had power over her.

But when she tried to move, to run after Felicity, her legs refused to budge. It was as if she'd been transported back to the night Uncle Ethan had approached her with the red-hot branding iron. Felicity had screamed her name, but Winifred hadn't been able to do anything except tremble and stare.

Now, as then, fear kept her rooted in place.

Chapter Thirteen

S OMETHING WAS WRONG with Marcus's livestock.

He might not have noticed it were it not for Winifred's blood restoring his heightened senses. His concoctions had always tasted awful, but the most recent mixture had a mildly spicy and sour flavor that could only have come from the blood itself. He lifted a vial to the flame of a candle on his workbench and tilted it back and forth so the thick liquid inside formed a film on the sides of the glass. Before Lucina's warning, he might have dismissed the change as inconsequential, but now he had to consider the possibility that the hunters were running a much subtler campaign than he'd expected.

What better way to weaken an adversary than to poison their food supply?

He was still considering that problem when his valet, Smith, arrived with his evening flask on a silver tray. The lean, wiry man wore his black hair neatly parted and slicked back with lemon-scented pomade, revealing a high forehead. He was in his early forties but had the weathered look of a man who had spent much of his life laboring beneath the sun.

He was also the only member of his staff other than Mrs. Gillanders and her husband, the butler, whom Marcus trusted with the secret of his nature.

Marcus waved the flask away. "The animals have been com-promised. Do not draw from them further."

Smith cleared his throat. "Shall I procure additional beasts from the village?"

Marcus shook his head. "If this is a hunter tactic, I do not wish to alert them."

He'd already had his groundskeeper check their wells and feed storage for any visible contaminants, but it was likely too late to discover the source of the problem. Whatever had been done to his livestock might already be affecting him. That would explain the sudden worsening of his symptoms.

He cracked the window open and poured his latest concoction out, then rubbed his temples with his thumb and forefinger. Perhaps Jonathan had been right, and it was time to draw the hunters out of hiding so they could begin a direct assault. Knowing they were nearby, possibly observing him within the walls of his own home, was not helping his already rattled nerves.

"There is another option," Smith said. "I would gladly bleed for you."

Marcus clenched his eyes shut. "No."

Drinking human blood might solve his immediate problem, but he had been down that road before, and he didn't like the creature that waited for him at the end. Too many innocents had died by his hand. He would not risk further death until he had ruled out every other possibility.

"Marcus?"

He spun around so quickly that he became dizzy and had to throw out his arms for balance. Winifred stood in the doorway behind Smith, looking as pale as a sheet. She glanced between the two men with her brow furrowed. "I-I did not intend to interrupt."

"You didn't," Marcus said quickly. "Please, come in."

Winifred stepped hesitantly through the threshold as Smith exited. Marcus did not miss the unusually penetrating look she gave the man. It was behavior he'd have expected between his quarreling brothers, not his wife and valet. But that was a concern for another day, as he had more than enough to deal with for the moment.

He wiped the sweat from his forehead with the back of his hand. Now that she'd come to him, he would attempt to rebuild the trust he'd damaged in the library.

"I owe you an apology. I should not have spoken to you so harshly earlier."

She was much more than a mere assistant. As much as he didn't want to admit it, he'd bedded dozens of men and women, but none had drawn out his protective instincts the way she did. He had practically strangled his own brother because Jonathan had suggested touching her. If the hunters had implanted her in his life as a spy or saboteur, they had chosen exceptionally well.

She stared at the wall. "Our guests have departed early."

"They have?" He hadn't expected them to leave for several days. "Why?"

Her jaw trembled. "Because I married you. My uncle said there is a feud between our families, and I chose my side."

It didn't make sense. He'd never even met any of her relatives before they'd arrived, as far as he knew. Perhaps Cordon had been right and the Belltree family was responsible for the murders in Glasgow and the defacement of the tavern in the village.

She wiped her damp cheeks. "My uncle won't even let me write to Felicity." Her voice broke on a sob. "I wish I'd stayed in Toronto."

His heart clenched. She would have had to have been a talented actress to fake such misery. Winifred's family was not above suspicion, but he could no longer believe she was plotting against him. Which meant she deserved even more of an apology than he'd delivered. He cupped her elbow. "Tell me how to make this right."

She rubbed her tears away. "Were you serious when you said you can't leave the castle?"

He sighed but could not regret telling her, given how many other lies he'd told. She deserved better than a husband who kept so many secrets. "Yes."

"Why?"

He took her hand and rubbed his thumb over her knuckles. That was a tough question to answer without revealing facts she was not prepared to learn. "It's… a long story."

"Marcus!" She jerked out of his grasp. "If I'm going to be trapped here with you, at least tell me why."

This wasn't how he'd wanted her to learn, but if it would appease her and salve his guilt for treating her so poorly, then he would tell her. "As you wish." He dragged two unvarnished spindle-backed chairs out of his pile of half-completed woodworking projects and set them in the middle of the room. "Please, sit. You've had an exhausting day."

She grasped the arched back of her seat and rattled it as if expecting it to fall apart before gathering her skirts and sitting with her hands folded in her lap and her back perfectly straight.

He matched her pose, took a deep breath, then began. "It started ten years ago. I'd prepared an invention to present at a symposium, a flask intended to keep liquids at a constant temperature through the application of vacuum force."

That was the closest he could get to the truth, that the event had been organized by vampires with the goal of finding new ways to operate in a human-dominated world without detection. He'd attended, intending to convince his peers that the biggest threat to their existence was their dependence on humans. He was proof that it was possible to sever that connection by consuming frequent small doses of animal blood, a task made easier using his flask.

"I was terrified, to be honest," he said.

Winifred scoffed. "You?"

He rubbed his damp palms along his trousers. "I've never been adept at speaking. Especially to people I don't know. Lucina—my youngest sister—was the one who encouraged me to attend. She escorted me down the line of chairs to the podium even as I was certain I'd fall over faint the moment I turned around and looked out at all those expectant faces."

He'd known his peers might reject his ideas. For many vampires, drinking from animals was disgraceful. It was akin to a wolf scavenging from what other predators left behind, a sign of weakness. He'd hoped that presenting the idea through a scientific lens would help his peers understand why they needed to adapt to the changing world to survive.

He'd been wrong.

"A member of the audience stood and called me a… a fraud."

Every time he closed his eyes, he returned to that moment, trembling before the man, with his long, black beard; dusty bowler hat; slicker coat; and gold-tipped cane. What the man had actually done was insinuate that Marcus could not hunt his own prey, a grave insult.

"No one rose to your defense?" Winifred asked.

"No."

He clenched his teeth as the most shameful part of that day returned in a flash.

"You would defile your body," the man said. "Did you get this idea from your maker?"

Marcus felt as if he'd swallowed a stone. His carefully constructed arguments vanished beneath the heckler's sneer. "M-Marguerite has n-nothing to do w-with this," he said as he shuffled through his notes. "W-Wh-When—" Something wet dripped out of Marcus's nose. He slapped his hand to his face as a murmur swept through the crowd.

"Wuh, wuh, wuh, what?" the man asked, in what was an obvious mockery of Marcus's stutter.

A sharp prickling started in Marcus's toes and swept up his body. He tried to speak, but the words wouldn't come. He was an embarrassment to his kind, a vampire rendered speechless by nothing more than cruel words. It would be better for his siblings if he walked into the sun and allowed them to be absorbed by other nests.

"The next thing I knew, I was lying on the ground."

He'd never learned the name of the man who'd stood up during his presentation, nor did he care. The awful thoughts that had assaulted him that day had made several reappearances over the following week, buzzing around his mind like irritating gnats. Unable to stand the noise in his own head, he'd fled to his family's ancestral castle.

The room fell silent, except for the howl of the wind outside and the crackle of the fire. He tilted his head back and stared at the patchwork of stones that made up the ceiling, not wanting to see the disgust or pity on her face. He was supposed to be the head of his family, the eldest of his nest, but was trapped in his own home. Were it not for Cordon and Jonathan visiting him every few months, he wouldn't have seen his siblings in years.

Marguerite would have been so ashamed.

The weight of his sorrow seemed to crush him into his seat, but he choked out a laugh. "I would give anything to walk freely in society again, but I fear it has been so long that I would not know what to do. It's become so bad that..." His throat tightened, but he forced himself to continue. "I have to follow a strict, regimented schedule because any amount of stress can trigger an attack."

It was like a barbed net had been dropped over his life that was slowly drawing tighter, forcing him to contort into increasingly uncomfortable shapes to keep from being sliced to pieces.

"So that is the aim of your experiments," Winifred said. "You're not treating your livestock. You're looking for a cure to your attacks."

He flushed. "Yes."

Her warm fingers touched the back of his hands. "What have you tried?"

He met her gaze. "Pardon?"

She gestured around them. "You've been here for a decade. Tell me what you've learned. Maybe I can assist you in finding a treatment."

He opened his mouth. Closed it. She wanted to help. After everything he'd done—failing to disclose his physical limitations before luring her to Scotland, rejecting her in the library when she'd been so earnest, causing her family to disavow her very existence.

He did not deserve her.

"I...I believe it is some manner of illness," he said. One unique to his species, although he would have to find a different way of approaching that subject. "I haven't identified the cause, although I suspect it is my diet." That would explain why none of his siblings were similarly afflicted. They subsisted on human blood. He'd never been more tempted to give up his prohibition, but each time he considered taking Smith up on his offer, he remembered the gurgling sound of his father dying after Marcus had torn out his throat in his fledgling rage.

"You said the attacks started after you were heckled?" Winifred asked.

He nodded, even as memories of blood-spattered windows and the cackling laughter of his gleeful maker crowded his thoughts.

She shoved to her feet and began pacing the room. "Consider the *Tusculanae Disputationes*. Cicero distinguished between worry regarding the future and a burst of emotion. *Angor*. In Latin, suffocation." She waved her hands, as if lecturing in front of an entire hall of students. "There are records of animals fleeing Helike in the days before a significant earthquake. To the citizens of the city, that behavior would have seemed irrational, until it wasn't."

Her sudden enthusiasm was amusing enough that it succeeded where he'd failed and banished the unpleasant echoes of his past to the depths of his mind. "What does my condition have to do with ancient Greece?"

She continued as if she hadn't heard him, walking faster as she spoke, as if growing excited by her theories. "The event itself wouldn't precipitate the attack. No, it would be anticipation. If we could interrupt the association—"

He caught her hand as she crossed his path for the fifth time. "Winifred. Slow down."

She blinked several times before smiling ruefully. "I apologize. When I get fascinated by a problem, I lose track of everything around me. What I am trying to say is, have you considered your attacks are a symptom of an illness not of the body, but of the mind?"

"I-I had not," he said, which was the truth. He did not want to offend her by dismissing her theory outright, but he could not believe any soul that had lived as long as he had could develop something as simple as a neurosis.

"You're skeptical," she said. "I can see it on your face." She put her hands on his shoulders. "But you've been at this for a decade. Give me a chance, Marcus. Let me try to help. My uncle won't listen to me, which means you are the only chance I have of ever seeing my cousin again. I need you healthy and able to fight, if need be."

His eyes burned with tears, but he refused to blink and let them fall. After so many years of trying to be like Marguerite and holding everything he felt tightly inside, he was no longer sure how to express emotion in a way that she would understand. He leaned his head so his icy cheek rested atop her warm fingers.

"As you wish."

Chapter Fourteen

WINIFRED CROSSED HER arms as she surveyed the bulging sacks slouched in the chairs that surrounded the narrow oak table she'd had the servants haul into the music room. "They don't look enough like people."

She'd considered using the dining hall, but it was far too cavernous. She needed Marcus to hear her without having to shout.

When she figured a way out of her uncle's decree and wrote to Felicity, she would leave out the details of this night. Her cousin would surely laugh if Winifred described her music room set for a formal dinner, except with the contents of the cook's pantry standing in for guests.

The butler, Gillanders, the housekeeper's husband, she'd learned, cleared his throat. "Hats, perhaps, my lady?"

Unlike Marcus's valet, Smith, Gillanders was a stout man with light-blond hair and a finely trimmed moustache. He spoke with a soft, reassuring voice and the skin around his eyes and mouth crinkled when he smiled, which was often.

She grinned. "That will do nicely."

As he left, Winifred walked to the nearest seat and plumped a bag of barley. Keeping busy helped her avoid thinking about the fact that she might never see her cousin again because of a feud Marcus insisted he knew nothing about. What she needed to do was have him speak to her uncle about the matter, as Uncle Ethan was much more likely to listen to a man than his own niece. Unfortunately, she doubted her uncle would make a return visit, which meant Winifred had to bring her husband to London.

Except Marcus couldn't leave the castle.

If there had never been a rivalry, as Marcus claimed, then that was the first problem she had to solve. He was so determined to find a solution to his attacks through scientific means, but the new knowledge she'd gained after spending the morning in the library made her believe a more effective approach could involve the principles of Hellenistic philosophy. In particular, a technique described by the Roman Stoic Seneca that involved focusing on the present when in periods of distress to maintain calm. Seneca also believed that suffering was necessary for growth, but that one should not become unhappy before a crisis arrived, as nothing in life was guaranteed.

Marcus had admitted that even thinking about going outside caused an immediate and powerful reaction. As she could not control his thoughts, she had to find a different way of eliciting the precise amount of stress necessary to bring on an attack without overwhelming him. After questioning him at length about what situations caused him anxiety, she'd chosen the easiest to replicate.

A dinner party.

Gillanders returned with several giggling maids carrying hat boxes. Winifred chose three to grace the "heads" of her guests. It was difficult getting them to remain in place, and she had to have a footman lash a few to their chairs to keep them from slouching, but it would have to do. She even chose a few necklaces from her jewelry box and draped them around the necks of the "ladies."

"What do you think?" she asked when she finished. Mrs. Gillanders looked ready to burst into laughter while her husband remained as silent and still as a statue. Only the faint twitching of his silver-speckled mustache gave away his mirth.

"I am not sure what you mean to accomplish, my lady," Mrs. Gillanders said in halting tones. "How is the master intended to interact with these…" She flicked a frayed edge of burlap.

"Guests?"

"It is only for practice. When he is comfortable with this, we can add other elements. Such as…"

"Dancing, my lady?" the butler asked.

Winifred nodded. "Precisely. Dancing, music, gossip. Those are all the things my husband needs to reacquaint himself with." They were also activities he could have engaged in at the wedding, but she'd assumed he'd been overwhelmed. She would venture to take him outside when he could successfully use the techniques she would teach him to manage these theatrical situations.

Gillanders smoothed his hands over the front of his jacket. "You could have the maids and footmen take the place of the guests."

She shook her head, having considered that option already. "He is much too accustomed to ignoring servants, and I would not ask them to pretend to be something they are not."

The soft click of heels from the hallway followed by the creak of a door opening made her turn. Marcus stepped inside, wearing a very fine black suit with a bowler hat tucked beneath his arm. It was almost as if he'd been warned. She turned to Gillanders and pouted. "You told his valet."

Gillanders tugged on the curly edges of his moustache. "Mr. Smith asked what we were preparing. I could not lie."

Marcus strolled forward, looking every inch the proper gentleman. He'd been handsome in his loose shirts and rumpled trousers, but if he'd approached her at a ball in Toronto dressed so fine, she would have swooned.

She licked her dry lips and began their evening charade by feigning that they were mere acquaintances and dipping into a curtsey. "My lord."

When she rose, he took her offered hand and kissed her fingers. "Your beauty has rendered me breathless, Miss Belltree. Your eyes shine like raging wildfires, and your chestnut curls are as perfectly tumbled as the earth after a landslide. When you enter a party, all eyes fly to your form as surely as the residents of a coastal city watching the horizon when the tide suddenly recedes."

His use of natural disasters to compliment her made her cheeks warm with pleasure. She flicked open the fan clutched in her other hand and waved it gently in front of her face. "Such flattery. Whatever would your wife say?"

She almost wished she'd met him in Toronto. Exchanging witty banter with him might have made those long nights in crowded ballrooms more bearable.

The skin around his eyes crinkled. "I am certain she'd agree. The countess and I share an appreciation for all that nature creates, both spectacular or devastating."

She barely suppressed a giggle.

Chapter Fifteen

"YOUR HAT IS, ah…fluffy," Marcus said to the sack of flour tilted precariously on the chair next to him.

"Thank you, my lord," Winifred said, in a squeaky falsetto.

He steadfastly kept his gaze on the lumpy bag. The last time he'd addressed Winifred instead of the "guest" with whom he was supposed to have been making polite conversation, she'd kicked his shin beneath the table.

"I am s-seeking a milliner. No, not a milliner. A, er…" What was the term? His grasp of language departed, leaving him tongue-tied before the contents of his cook's pantry, and his cravat became a noose around his throat. There were so many things he should have been doing. Continuing his experiments. Keeping his siblings from squabbling. Figuring out why hunters were lurking about. Preventing Winifred from figuring out why he slept through the day and rarely ate. He was capable of consuming food but did not enjoy the experience, as it often caused him to feel unwell for days after.

A repetitive clicking invaded his mind. His teeth were chattering.

If he didn't stop the hunters, he would be responsible for the next headless vampire that appeared. It might even be his Cordon, killed because Marcus had sent him to investigate. It would be as if he'd wielded a dagger and sliced it across his brother's throat himself. Blood would spray in an arc, splattering the dusty bricks on either side of the dark alley that was the scene of the ambush. The image was so clear in his mind that it felt like a memory.

A teacup rattled off the edge of the table and shattered on the floor.

"Breathe," Winifred said. "Then count, like I taught you."

Marcus inhaled slowly through his nose and out through his mouth.

One... two... three.

"Remember where you are," Winifred said.

Crouched in a dark alley far from the safety of his home, holding his brother's dying body in his arms. Cordon had called him, begged him to come, but Marcus had ignored the summons out of fear. Now it was too late. His siblings would never know how much he regretted pushing them away, even though it had been necessary to protect them.

"Marcus!"

He blinked and suddenly he was back in the music room. Winifred had come to his side and wrapped her fingers around his numb wrists.

She leaned closer. "There you are. You went somewhere else for a moment."

He forcibly relaxed the tense muscles of his shoulders and arms. Then a word came to him, like a bolt of lightning. "Hatter!" He slapped his palm on the table, making his cutlery shake. "I am seeking a hatter. Do you have a recommendation?"

"Well done," Winifred said. "Although I would suggest you do not strike the table next time. Mrs. Berry was so alarmed by your outburst that she spread a rumor across the *ton* that you imbibed too much wine and behaved inappropriately."

He wiped sweat from his forehead. The practice session Winifred had laid out had seemed laughable, but this was the fourth time he'd failed to get through the dinner with the Berry family, which included the gossipmonger Mrs. Berry (barley topped with a straw hat), her husband, Mr. Berry (flour lashed together with twine), and the soft-spoken Miss Berry (three pumpkins stacked in a pyramid, the topmost draped with a diamond necklace). The problem was the fictional Mr. Berry was nearly deaf, requiring Marcus to speak loudly for the man to hear, but Miss Berry startled at the slightest sound.

His heart still pounded from the attack, but at least he'd forced his way out of it. A small accomplishment, but one worth celebrating.

"Shall we try again?" Winifred asked.

He put his elbows on the table and his head in his hands. "I do not remember dinner parties being so wretched." Possibly because even before his involuntary confinement, he'd avoided socializing in favor of more scandalous events, much like Cordon. There had been a time when he'd taken his duties as a lord seriously, but that had been long ago.

Winifred sighed. "They usually aren't, but the entire purpose of this is to force you to manage your nerves." The screech of her chair being pushed back made him look up. She was adjusting Mr. Berry's body, which had slid to the point of nearly falling off his chair.

Marcus rubbed his handkerchief across the back of his neck, then balled it up and shoved it in his pocket. "You have succeeded. Where did you get the idea for this scenario, anyway?"

She paused in the motion of tilting Mrs. Berry's hat. "My parents invited a family very similar to the Berrys to dine with us. It was a miserable night. I had to hold my tongue a dozen times, and even then there were rumors spread the next day that I stormed off before the meal was complete." She chuckled. "It wasn't true, of course. I simply left the table the moment it was socially acceptable to do so."

He could imagine what that must have been like, with a woman as proper as the Mrs. Berry character. It had been years since he'd attended a social event. As much as he longed for a cure for his affliction, he was becoming increasingly aware that a life spent in solitude was not one worth living.

Winifred returned to her seat and picked up her wineglass by the stem. That was his signal that the scenario was beginning again.

"Mr. and Mrs. Berry enter with their daughter," Winifred said.

The room fell silent.

Winifred raised her voice. "I *said*, Mr. and—"

The footmen Winifred had roped into assisting them swung the doors open.

After several seconds, Marcus realized Winifred was watching and hurriedly stood. For the third attempt in a row, he'd nearly missed his cue. He walked to the front of the table and bowed. "Welcome, Mr. and Mrs. Berry."

"Why, thank you, my lord," Winifred said, in a comically deep voice. It had made him burst into laughter the first time he'd heard it. The woman was clever, humorous, and intelligent. He could hardly believe she cared enough to conjure up situations designed to help him.

He greeted the young Miss Berry and joined his guests at the table, all without earning a hiss from Winifred that would indicate he'd committed a social gaffe. The success criteria of this dinner party was to finish the night without embarrassing himself badly enough that Winifred judged the stuffy Mrs. Berry character would spread rumors the following evening. But if he focused his attention too much on charming her, then her jealous, hot-headed husband would challenge him to a duel.

It was, quite honestly, exhausting.

"This wine is atrocious," Winifred said as Mrs. Berry.

The first time Marcus had been given that prompt, he'd responded by defending his choice, but that route had inevitably led to failure. According to Winifred, Mrs. Berry's insults were intended to rattle him. Therefore, the correct response was to grin and not say or do anything that she could use against him.

"I will summon my butler to bring another," he said.

The rest of the dinner party played out as he expected, with Winifred only throwing in a few changes, as she did with each repetition, so as not to let him grow too comfortable. In this round, Mr. Berry loudly complained about the small portions and Miss Berry dropped her fan. For the former, Marcus instructed his butler to provide additional servings. For the latter, he was spared from failure when he reached down to grab the "fan" by Winifred, making a soft sound in the back of her throat. He quickly straightened and said, instead, "A footman notices the fan and fetches it for Miss Berry."

Winifred released a rush of air. "That was close."

Taking her words as a sign that the scenario was over, he slumped. "What would have happened if I had retrieved it?"

Winifred grinned. "Miss Berry would have accepted it and the moment your fingers brushed hers, she would have dropped in a faint."

He groaned. "I do not remember young ladies being so fragile."

Winifred fluffed her skirts. "Shall we go again?"

He wanted to say *yes*, but his backside was growing sore from sitting, there was a dull throb in his head, and he'd lost sensation in his fingers and toes.

She must have seen something in his face, because she walked around the table and put her hands on the back of his chair. "That's enough for today."

Something inside him that had wound tightly throughout the past few hours relaxed. Putting on an act in his own house was ridiculous, but it was surprisingly easy to forget it wasn't real. Winifred's voices and costumes made the characters come to life. He was solitary by nature, but he had to admit that he missed attending the occasional social event.

He put a hand on top of hers. "Thank you." Then he rose and kissed her fingers. "I eagerly anticipate our next session, my lady."

She lowered her gaze. "I find myself in an awkward position, my lord. I can recite poetry in Greek or Latin and have memorized the reported casualties of tsunamis and the maximum wind speed of several more hurricanes, but I have little understanding of what occurs between husbands and wives." She tilted her head. "Perhaps you could educate me?"

Marcus felt as if he were floating above his body. Winifred wanted him. He could hardly believe it. If not for his exhaustion, he would have stood and wrapped her in his arms. Unfortunately, his weakened state meant he could only abide the day for short periods. A vampire of his age should have had no difficulty remaining awake, but already, fatigue was settling on him, making it difficult to focus.

"I… cannot," he whispered.

He wanted to stay. Would have given anything to remain and continue their practice, or even better, drop to his knees and crawl beneath her skirts. He most looked forward to bringing her to completion with his mouth and hands and then again with his cock and fangs. The coppery scent of her blood wreathed around him and made his jaw ache.

But touching her when he was not fully in control was too dangerous. No matter how much he wanted her, he would not risk her life for one night of pleasure. Marguerite had not given him a choice before she'd taken him as her human lover and she hadn't even tried to be careful. If the worst happened with Winifred and he felt compelled to turn her, she might come to despise him, as he sometimes hated his maker.

She furrowed her brow. "Did I do something wrong?"

"Of course not. It is only that I… I have been alone for quite some time." It was a pathetic excuse, though not entirely a lie. He hadn't felt the kiss of a lover in years.

Her expression smoothed. "I see."

The waver in her voice belied her words. "Be patient with me, my dear."

"It's not that." She exhaled harshly. "I cannot believe I am admitting this, but… tonight has made me realize how much I miss people. A month ago, I resented my mother for dragging me to balls. Now I would give anything to host my own."

He brushed a stray curl away from her face. "I wish I could

give that to you."

She scrunched her nose. "Perhaps you can."

He wasn't sure he liked the sound of that. "What did you have in mind?"

"You could invite a few people from the village and introduce me as your wife. Consider it the next phase of practice."

He stiffened. "Allow strangers into the castle?" The wedding had been bad enough. Talking to objects was trivial compared to facing the real thing. If he failed and began stuttering or collapsed, the embarrassment might haunt and worsen his attacks.

"Only a few people," she said. "The vicar's family?"

He sighed. "If that is what you wish."

Chapter Sixteen

WHEN WINIFRED ARRIVED at the library the next morning, it was to the welcome sight of several new books piled on her usual table. As sunlight streamed over them, the air glittering with dust, a lump formed in her throat. There was no note, but she knew it was Marcus's doing, a very considerate act, given how she'd thrown herself at him the previous evening. She wasn't sure what surprised her more, that she'd been bold enough to ask him to teach her, or that he hadn't outright rejected her. Yes, he'd asked her to wait, but as a historian, she was well acquainted with time.

She shifted her skirts and settled down in her chair. She'd intended to continue the journal he'd read for her the previous evening, but she'd peruse the new volumes first. The book at the top of the stack had a worn leather cover and when she flipped it open, the text was hand-printed in medieval German. After puzzling over the vocabulary for several minutes, she realized it described a creature of the night similar to the ones her ancestors had supposedly hunted.

A vampire.

She set it aside and checked the next. It was as unusual as the first, again handwritten, but in French this time, and appeared to be another occult tome.

Why had Marcus selected these for her to read? They would have been better choices for Felicity. She would ask him the next time they spoke. Although, when they were alone, the parts of her mind that were insatiably curious quieted.

Three hours struggling to read scrawled German script later, she rubbed her temples with her fingers and stretched the stiffness out of her shoulders. She couldn't remember the last time she'd become so absorbed in any topic that was not at least tangentially related to a subject of her obsession. Usually, the only thing that piqued her interest enough that she slipped into a focus so intense that she lost track of time was natural disasters. She'd *tried* to engage her curiosity with several other subjects, but her mind inevitably refused to absorb any details. This was a fascinating development. She turned to a fresh page in her notebook and furiously jotted ideas.

> *Origin of vampire myth unknown. Modern depictions originate from Polidori's novel. Further sources required. Potential for investigation?*

She tapped the tip of her pencil on the paper. That was an interesting idea. She had assumed that when she sought publication to establish herself as a distinguished scholar, it would be for work relating to Pompeii. But what if she wrote about the creatures her family had supposedly once hunted instead? That would certainly be unique and might earn her good will from her uncle. Unlike her past proposals to publishers regarding volcanic eruptions or earthquakes, there would be less competition for a book on supernatural creatures. That would give her an advantage, especially if she could use Marcus's name. She had been dismissed out of hand countless times based on her sex alone.

Ideas for topics bloomed in her mind like weeds until a headache started and her wrist ached from clutching her pen. When she'd straightened and looked at what she'd written, her eyebrows rose. She had enough material for an entire series of textbooks. That should have been exciting, but she felt oddly morose.

Marcus's strange habit of sleeping through the day meant there were only a few hours each day when they were both awake. Was this to be her routine, alternating between silent, lonely meals in her room, assisting Marcus, and her research? It should have been a thrilling prospect, given how often she'd wished for more time to devote to her studies before she'd agreed to marry him, but faced with countless days of the same, there was a hollowness in the pit of her stomach.

It was difficult to immerse oneself in history when one was afflicted by homesickness.

Company, that was what she needed. It was time to circumvent her uncle's orders and contact her cousin. She returned to her room and rummaged around the drawers of her writing desk until she found the materials needed to compose a letter. Then she dipped her pen in ink and wrote.

> *My dearest Felicity,*
>
> *I wish you were here. This castle is gloriously large, but I find the many empty spaces make me quite lonely. I hope you will be reassured to know that married life has so far suited me, other than a few minor complaints. Solitude and study were exactly what I wanted, but I find there is something missing. Perhaps if I held a ball, you could pretend to be attending a country party and visit. I can hardly believe I am suggesting such a thing. Do you remember the time I begged a megrim for several days to finish reading Mommsen's first volume of* Römische Geschichte, *the History of Rome? Mother was furious when she learned the truth.*
>
> *As for Marcus, we are slowly learning about each other. If I had realized his peculiarities sooner, I might not have been so eager to travel here.*

She stopped, crossed out several lines, then crumpled the paper into a ball. She wanted to convince Felicity that she was well despite her uncle's orders, not have her cousin read the letter, then race out to a horse and ride across the country. Things were certainly not *that* bleak. She picked up another sheet of paper and tried again, this time aiming for a more positive tone.

> *Felicity,*
>
> *I hope this reaches you and that our uncle is treating you well.*

Please know that I will understand if you choose to not respond to prevent our uncle from punishing you. It pains me you were forced into making such an awful decision.

As for me, I have adapted well to married life. I have as much time as I wish to research and the earl even agreed that you can join me as my companion, although I fear we must settle the feud Uncle Ethan believes exists between our families before you can become my companion. Do you know anything about the conflict? I have asked my husband, but he could not provide clarity.

I miss you, and can't wait to see you again.

Winifred

After reading it several times, she found the tone stilting and awkward, but it would have to do. She folded the paper, sealed it with plain wax, and flipped it over. Her uncle would surely inspect any letter that arrived for his niece, but he would likely ignore the activities of his servants. She scrawled the name of Felicity's favorite maid, Anastasia. With luck, she would receive it, recognize who it was meant for, and route it to Felicity.

Winifred picked up the slim, blue leather book she'd brought from the library, hoping it would serve as a distraction. As soon as she'd opened it, she flushed. The first sketch depicted a naked man and woman sprawled on a couch, with the woman's face at the level of the man's crotch. Her mouth was clasped over his... Well, that was an interesting idea.

She was suddenly too hot to be wearing so many layers. Rather than summon Keenan, she struggled out of her dress, then found the wrapper she'd worn on her wedding night. The sleeves were rumpled and there were spots of grease on the bodice, but when she lifted the fabric, she could smell Marcus's sweat mixed with the lingering aroma of hot metal. She donned the garment, then returned to her bed and opened the book again. The next illustration made her spectacles fog. A man's head was buried between the thighs of a woman, who had her eyes closed and her mouth open. It was too easy to imagine the man as Marcus and herself as his lover.

They were married, but Marcus had not consummated their union. He'd asked her to be patient, but he'd also previously dismissed her as nothing more than his assistant. A suspicious part of her couldn't resist pointing out the unusual things she'd noticed. The rushed wedding. Spending most of the day asleep. The way he tensed when she touched him. The clues came together to form an answer she did not like but could not ignore.

Marcus had a mistress.

He must have been spending his days in *her* company and was only indulging Winifred because she had made her attraction so obvious. Her stomach tightened, but she had no right to be disappointed. Marcus was her husband, but their marriage was not a love match. Other than their first night, he had shown no interest in anything beyond companionship. It was her fault for misinterpreting his actions. If he wanted to take a mistress, she could not stop him.

She slammed the book shut, threw it across the room, then buried her face in her arms.

Chapter Seventeen

"*P*ERHAPS YOU COULD *teach me.*"

Winifred's whispered words echoed in Marcus's mind as he removed his leather apron from a peg on the wall in his workshop and donned it. She'd made her interest clear, but he'd foolishly not responded in kind. Instead, he'd offered a weak excuse that she'd inevitably question.

The problem was, every time he thought about kissing her, he remembered how he'd initially pursued Marguerite when he'd been human. If he'd known she'd been a vampire, he never would have gone willingly to her bed. She had deceived him in the same way he was deceiving Winifred. If he continued down the same path, he feared Winifred would come to resent him as much as he had Marguerite.

He carefully slotted vials of his latest concoction in the machine he'd decided not to destroy, even though it had harmed Winifred. Her practice session had given him a new insight into how he might confirm his suspicions regarding contamination in his livestock.

Before he saw her again, he would need to craft a believable explanation for his behavior. She was an intelligent, curious woman. If she hadn't already come up with her own theory, she would soon.

The truth would almost be easier, but he did not dare broach that subject until she'd had time to read the books he'd selected to educate her about his kind and was less likely to flee screaming from his presence.

It was not every day that one learned monsters were real.

He cranked his invention until it rattled, then released his tight grip, waited for the gears to slow to a halt, and opened the lid. To his surprise, the glass tubes tucked in the mahogany block had not shattered. When he lifted one, the cow's blood inside had separated into vague layers. He held it to a candle and inspected the topmost section. Unlike the samples he'd drawn from his animals several weeks prior and agitated, the cloudy liquid was not a pale yellow, but a faint pink.

It was the confirmation he'd been seeking, but it gave him no sense of satisfaction, especially because he didn't know how drinking tainted blood would affect him. Winifred's exercises were helpful in managing his attacks but did not explain how they had started. Given that they had worsened at the same time he'd discovered someone had tampered with his food supply, it seemed likely the hunters were responsible.

When he was too weak to fight back, they would stage their attack. If they were smart, they'd wait for his brothers to be present and pick them off one-by-one.

His head filled with static. He braced himself against his workbench and tried to remember that the situation was not yet dire. His enemy had infiltrated his pasture and coop, but there was one remaining source that was much harder to access.

The aviary.

It would be difficult to siphon only enough from his birds to sustain him while keeping them healthy, but the throbbing in his head and dryness of his throat told him he was running out of options. He exited his workshop and stumbled down the steps to a locked iron gate—thank God it was housed in the same tower— then shoved his hand in his pocket and removed a keyring. It took several painful seconds to force his unfeeling fingers to maneuver the correct key into the lock, but eventually, the latch made a reassuring click.

He turned the handle, shoved the rusty, metal gate open, and immediately knew something was wrong. The presence of a human should have elicited a riot of screeching, but it was unnaturally silent.

"No," he whispered. "Please, no."

Several more steps and the cause became clear. The cages were open and every bird, from the smallest dove to the largest eagle, had been torn apart. It was such a grisly scene that his first thought was that a wolf had somehow breached the castle, but that was absurd. The room had been locked, and the window was too high for any four-legged creature to reach.

He clenched his shirt over his heart. It felt like he was caught in the grip of an enormous, constricting snake. His animals were all that kept him from regressing into bloodlust and attacking his staff. If he couldn't find a solution, the castle might become the scene of a slaughter worse than the one he'd caused in his village shortly after being turned. Smith, Gillanders, Mrs. Gillanders, and even Winifred would have no chance of stopping him. One after another, he would tear out their throats, drain them dry, and leave their limp, discarded bodies for his siblings to find when they next visited.

He crumpled to his knees onto a pile of rotten turnips and clenched his teeth until his jaw ached. The sense of doom that had him imagining violent, awful futures for the people under his protection was nothing more than a trick of his mind. The latest symptom of the affliction that had taken his freedom, independence, and pride. He rifled through his memories until he recalled Winifred's calming voice during his attack in the music room.

"Breathe."

He inhaled through his mouth until his lungs were full to bursting, then exhaled powerfully through his nose.

"Remember where you are."

Inside the castle aviary, kneeling on a sticky floor.

The weight in his chest eased, and he rose unsteadily to his feet. Impending sunrise meant it was time for him to retire, but first, he would tell the groundskeeper to set snares and traps. The blood of a few rabbits or a dozen rats wouldn't satisfy him for long, but it was preferable to starvation.

Chapter Eighteen

WINIFRED FOUND MARCUS standing outside the closed doors to the dining room, staring at the carved mahogany panels as if they were the gates of hell and the handles were hissing cobras. Part of her wanted to demand to know if he'd taken a mistress. But that would likely only worsen his anxiety, and if she was going to figure out how to convince Uncle Ethan there was no feud and see Felicity again, she needed him able to leave the castle.

"I'm here," she said. Then she removed a handkerchief from her pocket and tucked it between the thumb and index finger of his right fist.

"Thank you," he said. Without looking at her, he dabbed the soft fabric against his skin. "I-I do not know if I can do this. When I get anxious, I can barely eat."

"You can. We will say you are recovering from illness."

If she'd thought him truly not ready, she would have sent him away and made up an excuse to placate her guests, which included the vicar, his wife, and their two young daughters. But Marcus had insisted an hour earlier that she not allow him to retreat. It was only a momentary burst of fear that had paralyzed him.

She still thought it odd that a man of science, an inventor, seemed incapable of conquering the metaphorical demon that plagued him. "You need not say much," she said as a footman opened the door from the inside. "I will lead the conversation."

The space was lit by several hanging chandeliers and a long table was set up in the middle of the room, where the guests were already sitting. The vicar, Mr. Charles Benton, was gesturing to the large windows. His wife, Winona Benton, nodded every few seconds, making the peacock feathers tucked in her silver-blonde hair bob. Their two daughters tilted their brown, curly heads together and whispered.

"Give me your arm," Winifred whispered.

Marcus did so, and she placed her fingers on his sleeve. He led her to her seat, then took his, but when he sat, the table fell silent.

As if on cue, six servants filed in, carrying small, white plates containing grapefruit halves on trays.

"We were surprised to receive your invitation, my lady," Mrs. Benton said. She spoke softly, but the intensity in her bright-blue eyes and the way she kept her back perfectly straight reminded Winifred of her mother. This was not a woman to be trifled with. She turned to Marcus. "Will you and the countess be having more events in the future, my lord?"

Winifred tensed. That was not a question they had practiced.

"That is up to my wife to decide," Marcus said after only the slightest hesitation.

She forced her stiff shoulders to relax. He'd successfully navigated his first hurdle. The vicar and his wife were easy guests to entertain. They expected very little, and unlike proper society, would not notice or care if Marcus used the wrong spoon or rambled about a subject for far longer than necessary. It also helped that Mrs. Benton had raised her twin daughters to be both polite and kind. Over the next hour, Mrs. Benton made several comments that led Winifred to suspect she wanted Winifred to become friends with the girls. Likely to improve their social standing. Winifred was happy to do so, although she doubted association with her would hold much sway in the village.

Mr. Benton finished the last of his roast partridge, set down his fork, and patted his stomach. "That was magnificent."

"Indeed," Mrs. Benton said. "I only wish you had invited us to your table sooner, my lord."

Marcus froze. Winifred sensed the exact moment panic set in.

You can do this. It was a joke, not a critique.

He lifted a glass to his lips, a tactic she had shown him during their sessions, allowing him a few more seconds to respond. Then his cutlery began to bounce.

"Our cook is remarkable," she said loudly. "I will pass along your praise, Mrs. Benton. The ginger cream is my favorite." She dipped her spoon in a bowl that contained a rich dessert flavored with strawberries and redcurrant jelly, then brought the dessert to her mouth. The entire time, she watched Marcus out of the corner of her eye. Judging from the way he subtly repositioned the silverware next to his plate, he was through the worst of the attack.

The rest of the meal proceeded without incident, and soon they were standing in the entryway alone, aside from a bored-looking footman.

"That went well," Winifred said.

Marcus scoffed. "I would not call it a rousing success." There were bags under his eyes and his face was sweaty. "I have not had such a stressful evening in decades. At least I was able to exit the wedding celebration early."

She put her hands on her hips. "I remember."

He grinned. "Thank you. For tonight. I appreciate it."

"You do not need to pretend. I know you hated every minute."

He put his palm over his heart. "You wound me. I merely *disliked* every minute."

She matched his grin and remembered how Felicity had warned her that there was more to him than he presented. Her cousin could not have known how right she had been. Winifred had married him because she'd wanted the freedom to pursue her research. She hadn't expected him to slip between her ribs and wrap around her heart like a soft blanket. It was with that in mind that she twined her arms around his neck.

He stiffened and maneuvered out of her grasp. "Not tonight."

She let him go, even as she felt her heart breaking. He'd asked for time, but that could be a delaying tactic. She didn't want to believe he had a mistress, but all the evidence pointed to the conclusion she'd arrived at the previous night.

Marcus was in love with someone else.

Chapter Nineteen

November 29th, 1867, Scotland

MARCUS AWOKE FEELING as if he'd been thrown off a mountain and tumbled all the way down. Every muscle in his body ached, and his mouth tasted like he'd swallowed a handful of sand. He'd dreamed of Winifred, that he'd swept her in his arms and kissed her instead of letting his fear push her away. For more than three weeks, she'd found ways to avoid him, by sleeping through most of the night and taking her meals in her room. He'd tried to ask what was wrong, but the words never came out right. The problem was he'd spent so many years keeping his siblings at a distance to maintain the hierarchy in the nest that he didn't know how to manage the intensity of emotion Winifred elicited in him. The easiest thing to do was bury it deep in his mind, so that was what he did.

He ran his hand through his hair and felt something wet. When he looked at his fingers, they were bloody. He flipped the blankets off his nude body and gasped. From his nipples to his knees, he was covered in angry, red welts. He struggled out of bed and tugged the rope to summon his valet. When Smith showed up five agonizing minutes later, he carried a tray holding a silver flask, which he placed on the floor before backing up several steps.

It was the right thing to do. Despite Marcus's vow not to bite him, his mouth watered as he imagined the pulsing veins in Smith's throat. It would be so easy to overpower him. Then Marcus could sink his fangs deep and drink until his strength returned. Biting anywhere would do, although the most pleasurable way to drain a victim was the femoral artery. His gaze dropped to his valet's trouser-clad thighs before he closed his eyes and forced the unwanted thoughts away.

"My lord?" Smith asked as he edged toward the exit.

"Leave," Marcus said. "I cannot... My control is not what it should be."

Smith quickly obeyed.

Marcus grabbed the flask, unscrewed the lid, and sipped the lukewarm liquid inside. The pungent flavor told him it was deer, but the slightly spicy aftertaste stopped him from drinking further. He didn't know how, but it was tainted. The hunters had bested him again. He'd intended to spend the night investigating how they had gained access to his aviary, but now the thought of getting out of bed was almost too much to bear. Nor could he risk seeing Winifred. It was far too dangerous. He wasn't strong enough to resist the allure of her smile, her kindness, her intoxicating scent.

He buried his head in his pillow. Winifred seemed convinced that his problem was in his mind, but his new symptoms disproved that theory. The fact that he'd yet to determine the cause of the contamination in his animals did not help. That brought him back to his invention. The only difference between the blood he'd pulled several weeks ago versus recently was the topmost section he'd observed after agitation. If it contained the toxin, perhaps all he had to do was remove it. That would require adjustments to his machine to reach higher speeds and create cleaner divisions. Otherwise, the toxin might leech into the other components and render his effort futile.

He struggled to his feet and over to the secret door that led to a corridor he could use to reach his workshop with no one seeing him. Cordon would be furious if he discovered he'd worked while in such poor shape, but he could not give up.

The following few hours passed in a haze of frustration as he disassembled his invention, adjusted the gears, then slotted it back together. When the machine was finally ready to operate, his joints popped and crackled with every movement and the wounds on his arms oozed a foul-smelling liquid. They healed quickly enough, only to form new welts, as if his flesh were a simmering pot of water.

He carefully divided the rest of the blood from the flask Smith had brought him into vials, slotted them into the block of wood, then clasped the handle and turned. It was tremendously difficult, but he continued for as long as he was able, then waited for the machine to stop and opened the lid with trembling fingers.

A crimson mess awaited him. He'd spun too fast, and the fragile vials had cracked. He fell to his knees and buried his head in his hands. Another failure. He would have to ask Smith to draw from his cattle, even if it would make his condition worse.

He shoved his mechanism over, sending it crashing to the ground. Liquid oozed out of the top and pooled on the floor. He didn't care. He lurched his shaking body out of his workshop and down the steps. When he reached the third floor, he ran face-first into his valet.

"You should not be out of bed," Smith said.

Blood. Fresh human blood inches away from his face. He rasped his tongue along Smith's neck before the fog in his mind cleared. Then he shoved his valet away and braced himself against the wall. "Get away."

The idiotic man did not flee. He tugged off his cravat and exposed his neck. "Drink."

Marcus's fangs throbbed. He leaned closer and brought his lips to Smith's warm flesh but stopped short of biting. He'd made a vow to not consume human blood.

A vow he'd already broken by tasting Winifred the night of their wedding.

And he was *so thirsty.*

"Drink, my lord," Smith said. "I rather enjoy this position and would prefer you do not perish."

The last of Marcus's resistance vanished. He plunged his teeth into Smith's neck and let his mouth fill with the achingly familiar taste. With each swallow, the sharp edges of his thoughts smoothed. It was like he was a powder-dry sponge uncurling from a twisted and malformed shape as he absorbed precious fluid.

He would owe Smith a significant debt, which he would repay with a generous bonus and a letter of recommendation if he wished to leave the castle after having such an awkward encounter with his employer.

A soft gasp made him look up.

Winifred was standing in the hall with her hands over her mouth.

He licked the blood from his lips and teeth before lifting his head from Smith's neck.

She stumbled backward, slipped on her skirt, then tumbled to the ground.

"Winifred!" He ran to her, fell to his knees, and placed her head on his lap. His valet was calling out his title, but he didn't care. She'd seen his true nature and had reacted exactly as he'd feared. When she awoke, she would surely flee the castle, leaving him alone again.

"My lord!"

Marcus looked up. The wound on his valet's neck was gone, healed by Marcus's saliva. Smith was slightly paler but showed none of the fear Marcus had seen in Winifred's expression.

"What shall I do with the countess?" Smith asked.

Marcus stared for several seconds before realizing Smith meant Winifred. The Countess of Kingsberry. His wife. Who had seen him biting his valet. It wasn't as if he'd intended to keep his nature a secret forever—he'd selected books intended to introduce her to vampirism—but for her to find out in such a way… A vise formed around his chest. If she fled, she might attract the attention of the hunters. He couldn't allow it. But the idea of locking her up like a prisoner made him sick to his stomach.

"Shall I return her to her room?" Smith asked. "I could speak to her. Explain that you did me no harm."

Marcus ran a hand through his hair. "Ah…no. Leave it to me."

Smith rubbed his hands together and shifted on his feet.

"Stop fretting." Marcus gathered Winifred in his arms. Rising proved a greater challenge, but he pushed through the lingering ache in his thighs until he was back on his feet. Only then did Smith depart.

Marcus proceeded slowly toward Winifred's room, not wanting her to awaken in his arms after her shock. His strength should have been completely restored after consuming so much human blood, but his right knee made an unpleasant clicking sound with each step.

At least the hunger that had churned in his gut was gone and he could think clearly once again. He had to offer Winifred answers, but first he had to give her a reason to stay. As he would not force himself into her presence, that meant finding some other way to communicate.

They had started with letters, so that was how he'd proceed. When he arrived at her room, he laid her gently atop the bed. She looked so peaceful in slumber that he dared to touch his lips to her temple. Then he grabbed a sheet of paper from a drawer in her desk and hurriedly scrawled out the words that poured from his heart, not bothering to correct any mistakes or clean smudges when he accidentally drew his thumb across freshly written ink.

She did not stir once, although he paused several times to anxiously confirm she was still breathing easily. He told himself he did this out of concern for her welfare, but it was also a stalling tactic. After he left, he might never see her again.

It was likely she would not understand what she'd seen. She would be confused and frightened and would expect him to act like a monster. What he needed to do was remind her he was the same man she'd traveled across the ocean to marry. Once she understood that, and the importance of not revealing his secret, he would offer her freedom. It would shatter what was left of his heart, but he had orchestrated his death before and would do so again if necessary.

He placed the finished letter on her desk, then checked on his beautiful, brave Winifred once more. She'd drooled on her pillow and there was a faint scent of blood, likely from an abrasion acquired during her fall, but her pulse was steady. He longed to remain at her side, but she deserved a chance to recover from what she'd seen in privacy.

Her spectacles had tumbled to the floor. He placed them atop her commode, then forced himself to exit the room. As the door closed, he leaned his forehead against it and sighed.

"Quite a mess," Cordon said.

Marcus faced his brother. "How long have you been watching?"

Cordon narrowed his eyes. "You do me a disservice, brother. I arrived mere moments ago. Smith told me what occurred."

Marcus was torn between relief and embarrassment. The former because he had never felt so alone and the latter because he hated Cordon knowing that his brother had lost control. At least Smith's donation had strengthened him, although he didn't feel nearly as powerful as he had after consuming a single drop of Winifred's blood.

Yet another way she was different. That was a mystery he would attempt to solve after the crisis ended.

"What will you do if she runs?" Cordon asked.

"She will not."

Cordon put a hand on Marcus's shoulder. "You threaten our existence."

"Did you not do the same when you told Katherine?"

Cordon scowled. "Kitty knew what I was before we married. Had she balked when I told her I was a vampire, I could have asked Seraphina to erase her memories and there would have been no record of our relationship. You cannot say the same for you and Winifred." He ran a hand through his hair. "You are behaving recklessly, brother. It is not like you."

"Do not test me," Marcus said. He'd given his younger brother more chances than he would have allowed from any of his other siblings out of guilt for not joining Cordon when his brother had thought he'd been dying. But the disrespect could not continue.

Cordon tightened his grip. "You aren't thinking clearly."

Marcus's patience snapped. He forced his blood through his palm until it formed a scarlet dagger, then spun around and pressed the blade against Cordon's throat. He might regret fighting his brother later, but the turmoil raging inside him made it easy to set those concerns aside.

Cordon's eyes turned a vibrant blue but dipped his head. "I apologize. I overstepped."

"Allow me until sunrise to speak to her," Marcus said as the dagger melted back into his palm. "If, after that, you still believe she is a threat, then I will summon Seraphina."

Neither he nor his brother could erase so many of Winifred's memories, but their eldest sister possessed that skill. Marcus had not called upon her to use her talent for decades, but he would not hesitate to do so if Winifred threatened his family.

"She will fear you," Cordon said.

Marcus strolled past his brother and descended the steps. "I know."

Chapter Twenty

WINIFRED PUSHED UPRIGHT and rubbed the bridge of her nose with her thumb and forefinger. She was back in her bedroom, tucked beneath her silk sheets with a damp spot on her pillow. Her dream had been awful. She'd wandered the castle in search of her husband, only to find him embracing Smith with his lips to the man's throat. She struggled out of bed and felt a sharp twinge in her back from where she'd collapsed on the stone floor of the hall.

It hadn't been a dream.

Marcus was in love with his valet.

And on top of everything, when she pulled herself into a sitting position, there was a red stain on her sheet. Her monthlies had arrived.

She put her hands over her face to muffle her cry. She couldn't be angry with him. He had been extraordinarily upfront with his intentions. Now that she understood his preference, she would maintain a professional distance. There was no other choice. Her family wanted nothing to do with her. Even if she convinced Marcus to agree to an annulment on the grounds that they had not consummated the marriage, he couldn't leave the castle and, therefore, couldn't appear before a magistrate to provide testimony.

She was trapped.

The world seemed to shrink around her. She squeezed her eyes shut. Falling into despair would accomplish nothing. Before leaving Toronto, she had accepted her future in a marriage of convenience. What did it matter that Marcus did not love her? She'd never expected it from him. It was her own feelings for him that were the problem.

She exhaled slowly. He never had to know. She might mourn a life she'd never known she'd wanted, but she still had the resources Marcus had promised. She had a home, a comfortable position, and the time to do anything she wished. Her uncle might have forbidden her from corresponding with her cousin, but Felicity was far too clever not to find a way around that rule. At worst, she would break free when she came of age. All was not yet lost. She wiped tears from her face, grabbed her spectacles from the table beside her bed, and moved to her dressing table to clean herself up. A few minutes later and with a napkin attached to a belt tucked beneath her skirts, she felt ready. She would not let this revelation stop her from continuing her research.

Her hands shook as she turned her doorknob, but when there was no one waiting outside, she relaxed.

"What were you expecting?" an unfamiliar voice asked.

She jerked her head around. A man in a silver-and-black striped suit and trousers leaned against a pillar. He looked so much like Marcus that she felt a jolt of panic until he stepped forward and put his hands in his pockets. Then she realized his complexion was not nearly so pale, and he was much taller and sturdier than her husband. It was Marcus's brother Viscount Grayson.

Winifred curtseyed, even though she outranked him. "Good evening, Lord Grayson."

He sniffed. "My brother thought you might have… questions."

Winifred held up her hands. "I assure you I do not!" The law might have considered Marcus's actions illegal, but she knew there were historical records of similar couples going back millennia. "I am not one to judge who he loves."

Lord Grayson's expression changed. One second, he looked

like a prison guard prepared to barricade her in her room; the next, he gaped like she'd told him she wanted to *join* Marcus and his valet in their bedchamber.

"Tell me," Lord Grayson said as he sauntered closer. "What do you believe you saw before you collapsed?"

"I do not wish to repeat it."

"Indulge me."

Her cheeks burned. "You are trying to intimidate me."

He wagged his eyebrows. "Is it working?"

She grinned. She couldn't help herself. Despite their physical similarities, the man was entirely different from her husband. Whereas Marcus was shy and reserved, Cordon was confident and flirtatious.

"Tell me what you saw," Lord Grayson asked again.

It was as if he'd slipped into her mind and set her reservations aside. "M-My husband embracing a-and kissing his valet's neck."

"That is all?"

He sounded both relieved and amused, which made her wonder if there had been something else. For a moment, as she'd stared at Marcus's face, she'd thought his teeth had been... She shook her head. Dwelling on the memory would only further upset her.

She stepped back into the room to avoid any servants hearing. "I know what I saw." Then, to her horror, a tear dripped down her cheek. She spun around and dashed it away with the back of her hand. That was when she noticed the envelope sitting the letter on her desk. Before she could reach for it, Cordon sprinted past her—how had he moved so fast?—and snatched it. "My lord!" She scowled. "Isn't that for me?"

"No." Lord Grayson tucked the envelope into his jacket. "Well, yes, but you are not ready to read it." Then he winced.

"Yes. No. Why?" He shook his head. It was distinctly odd, like watching him have a conversation she could not hear. She stepped back toward the door, hoping Lord Grayson would follow her out. She trusted Marcus, but she knew very little about his brother.

Lord Grayson clicked his tongue. "My wife would like to speak with you." He walked to the door and held it open. "She is coming."

Winifred followed his gaze. A woman was ascending the stairs. She raised her arm and waved, sporting an enormous grin. It was disarming, and perhaps that was her intent, as Winifred immediately relaxed.

The viscountess had long, brown hair piled atop her head in an elaborate chignon and wore a dark-blue, fitted day dress with long sleeves and a square neckline that revealed a startling amount of pale skin. The fabric was embroidered with silver stars and moons that flowed seamlessly from her bodice to her skirt, which was trimmed with several inches of silver lace. She hurried up the stairs and down the hallway, then joined her husband's side, her cheeks flushed and eyes wide.

"My lady. I've been looking forward to meeting you again. You must call me 'Kitty.'"

It took Winifred several seconds to realize the woman was referring to her. She was entirely unaccustomed to having a title. She dipped into a curtsey—again unnecessary, as she outranked the viscountess—then rose to find Lord Grayson whispering to his wife. Kitty's cheeks had reddened, and the skin around her eyes was crinkled, as if she were trying to hold in laughter.

Winifred was about to ask what they were discussing, when Cordon straightened. "I'll leave you two alone."

He had barely taken two steps before Kitty swept past Winifred. "When Cordon told me Marcus was to be married, I admit I was skeptical. Marcus has always been so..." She sniffed. "Analytical."

Winifred smiled. "He *is* an inventor."

The countess grinned. "Oh, yes. Cordon and I rely on several items he designed." She clapped her hands. "Now, show me your closet. While I am here, I should see what I am working with."

Twenty minutes later, a bemused Winifred stood with her

arms outstretched as Kitty crouched in front of her and examined the skirt of her best gown. Despite what Winifred had expected, Kitty did not speak further about Marcus. Instead, she regaled Winifred with the surprisingly charming story of how she'd met her husband. Winifred had to clap a hand over her mouth when Kitty got to the part about Lord Grayson stealing a scarf from her pocket, then brazenly wearing it to her shop. Winifred had only known the man for a few minutes, but she could easily imagine him tempting Kitty into helping him complete the list of scandalous tasks Kitty described.

"There," Kitty said as she drew her needle through a tear in the velvet gown she'd insisted on repairing, even though Winifred had assured her it was unnecessary, and the duty of a lady's maid. Winifred got the impression that it was easier for Kitty to converse when her hands were busy.

Winifred could relate. She respected the viscountess for continuing to pursue her passion even after marriage.

"I know relatively little about your husband," Kitty said. She put her pins, needles, and thread back in the metal box she removed from her pocket. "But I can say he does not show emotion easily. I daresay he cares for you a great deal."

Winifred's smile fell. "Our marriage is one of convenience. If he is in love with another—"

"Nonsense," Kitty said. "Do not make assumptions without proof. You believe Marcus has an arrangement with his valet. I am here to tell you that is not true."

Winifred shifted on her feet. She wanted to believe it, but if Marcus was not involved with Smith, then what had they been doing embracing?

Bloody fangs and impossibly bright-blue eyes.

She shook her head, dismissing the image. The occult books Marcus had left for her were polluting her memories. The only thing she'd witnessed in the hallway had been a liaison, nothing more.

"Do you want my advice?" Kitty asked.

Winifred ran her palms over the soft fabric of her bodice. "Yes, please."

"Don't trust your memory. Ask him directly."

That logic was hard to dismiss.

Chapter Twenty-One

WINIFRED HATED HIM. That was the only reason Marcus could come up with to explain why his brother had not yet returned. Winifred should have read his letter by now. She must have recoiled such that Cordon had spirited her out of the castle, far away from the monster she'd married.

He stopped pacing and collapsed into his favorite chair by the fireplace. Damn his brother for taking so long. The waiting was worse than torture. However, getting himself worked up wouldn't help. If Winifred agreed to speak with him, he would have to be extremely careful to keep his distance and do whatever it took to avoid frightening her. That was his only chance of convincing her not to flee.

Oh, God, he didn't want her to go. The thought of returning to the lonely routine he'd established before she had entered his life, first with her charming, sprightly letters, and then with her glorious presence, was tremendously depressing. It was as if he'd existed two centuries with part of his soul missing and hadn't realized it until Winifred had appeared. She was the beating heart at the center of his world. Losing her was more than he could bear.

He had to hope she felt even a fraction of the overwhelming affection he held for her.

His pacing was interrupted by an envelope slipping beneath his door. When he picked it up, he felt his eyebrows rise. It was the one he'd left for Winifred. His fingertips began to tingle. Was this her way of rejecting him? Was she so terrified that she could not bear to look at him?

He turned the envelope over and laughed. The words "good luck" were scrawled on the back in Cordon's distinctive, messy handwriting.

Good luck with what? Convincing Winifred not to leave? Had she given the letter to Cordon to return because she could not bear to face him? He opened the door, but his brother was nowhere to be seen. It was typical of Cordon, expressing his disapproval that Marcus had not summoned Seraphina to erase Winifred's memories in such a strange way. He shoved the envelope into his pocket and returned to pacing.

"Marcus?"

He started. Apparently, he'd been so absorbed in his thoughts that he hadn't heard Winifred enter. She stood in the doorway, with Cordon's wife behind her. Kitty was grinning, but Winifred looked cautious. That was far better than the fear he'd expected. Either she'd decided to give him a chance to explain, or Cordon had taken the letter before she'd read it for unknown reasons. Perhaps it was foolishly optimistic, but he chose to assume the former.

He clasped his hands in his lap and launched into his practiced speech. "If you wish to leave the castle, a carriage is already prepared and waiting. I will understand if you can't live…with…"

Kitty was shaking her head furiously and mouthing the word "no."

Winifred glanced over her shoulder. "Thank you for accompanying me, Kitty, but I would like to speak to my husband privately."

Kitty inclined her head. "Of course. I have no doubt Marcus will explain his *relationship* with his *valet* to your satisfaction."

He gulped. If he understood Kitty's message correctly, Winifred had somehow convinced herself he'd had taken Smith as his lover. That explained her lack of fear. She must not have read his letter, after all.

"Please, sit," he said.

She straightened her shoulders. "Are you in love with Smith?"

The question was so absurd that he laughed. It was the entirely wrong thing to do, judging from the flush that crept up her neck.

"No," he said before she could misinterpret his response. "Smith is a loyal servant. Nothing more."

Her shoulders drooped. "Then what were you..."

He gestured to the seat across from him. "Sit. Please."

She walked over to the chair and then sank into it like a deflating balloon. "I feel so foolish."

He chuckled. "I am the one who should be apologizing. Let me set the record straight. I have not taken a lover in more than a decade." He paused, licked his lips, then added, "Not that I would be averse to sharing pleasure with a man. Or multiple men. Or several men and women at the same time." He shrugged. "I am not particular."

Her face had become so red, he feared she would faint again. At least she sat close enough that he could catch her if she tumbled over.

"What you saw," he continued in a softer tone, "was nothing more than Smith supporting me as I collapsed after working for too long without a break."

He did not like lying to her, but for whatever reason, her mind was electing not to remember certain details from what she'd witnessed. Until she was ready to accept the truth of his nature, he would keep it from her.

She furrowed her brow. "You shouldn't have been in your workshop without me."

He leaned back. That was certainly not a response he'd expected. She'd gone from embarrassed to chastising in record time. It was, he admitted, rather nice to have someone trying to "mother" him. The only other person he'd ever allowed to speak to him in such a way was his nest sister Helena. She was the most sensitive of his siblings, the keeper of their family archives, and the only one of them with medical training, having been a nurse before Marguerite had chosen her to join their family.

"The letter on my desk," Winifred said. "Was it from you?"

The muscles in his neck twitched. "Ah, well, yes." Then, before she could ask about its contents, "I left it to explain the...misunderstanding. In case you did not want to speak to me."

It wasn't true, but he could not give her the letter now. She was obviously not ready to learn the truth of his vampirism.

She tilted her head and raised her eyebrows. "Why would Lord Grayson take it from me?"

"Perhaps my brother wanted you to hear the explanation from me directly?" He brushed his hand over the pocket that held the envelope. "I admit I have a habit of losing myself in my work rather than facing conflict."

"Marcus," Winifred said, in a sharper voice. "I want you to promise you won't continue your experiments unless I am there to help."

He grinned. "I promise." He'd tried nearly every combination of blood possible with limited results, anyway, and the infusion from his valet would ease the worst of his symptoms. In fact, with his thirst sufficiently satisfied, his other urges made themselves known most insistently. Now that he no longer had to fear losing control, there was no reason to stay away from his wife. He could banish any suspicions she might have developed because of his prior restraint and show her exactly how much he desired her. He rose slowly, observing her face for any sign of fear, then crouched in front of her and clasped her hands. "There is something I want to ask."

A fizzing sensation started in his stomach. He was not capable of becoming intoxicated, but every time he touched her, it felt as if she'd drunk several gallons of mulled wine. "B-Before," he started, "you s-said... After we..." His throat worked. "I apologize. I have been alone for too long and am having difficulty finding the words to express myself."

She placed her other hand on top of his. "Take your time."

He licked his dry lips. "We had agreed in our letters that our marriage would be one of convenience, and I will not ask more of you. However…" He threaded their fingers together. "Am I correct in assuming that you did not find my touch entirely repellant?"

"You are correct," she whispered.

"W-What about this?" he asked. He caressed her palm with his thumb. "Is this…acceptable?"

She arched her body like a pampered housecat. "Yes."

"And this?" He leaned forward and touched his lips gently to hers.

She flinched. He started to pull back, when she looped her arms around his neck. He took that as a positive sign and tilted his mouth, bringing their lips apart and then together again. Every place his skin touched hers sparked with sensation.

He longed to draw her warm, soft body close and make her cry out his name, but this was new to her, so he would let her control how slow or fast they moved forward. Then her wandering fingers touched the bulge in his trousers, sending a bolt of pleasure through him that jostled his senses back in order. It was too soon after her shock. She deserved a better setting to experience her first time.

He repositioned her hand on his trousers to her shoulders. "Winifred…"

She huffed. "I wish you would not do that. I'm not fragile. You won't break me."

"I am not so sure of that."

She pressed her lips to the corner of his mouth. "Trust me."

"Winifred," he whispered between her closed-mouthed kisses. "We should discuss this before we proceed. You are innocent."

The urge to extend his fangs grew with every passing second, but he tamped down his vampiric instincts with every bit of his strength. He would only go as far as she wished, which did not include sampling her blood a second time.

No matter how much pleasure it would have brought them both.

"No more talking," she said. "Touch me, Marcus."

It was a plea he could not deny. He slid his hands beneath her skirts and massaged her thighs above her stockings while dragging the tip of one fang along her throat. A fraction more pressure, and his saliva would render her boneless. He could fill his mouth with her blood and drink as much as he desired. It had been mere hours since Smith's donation, but the craving burned in him as if it had been years. There was a flask waiting on the table next to his bed, but the mere thought of letting the thick, cold liquid slide down his throat filled him with revulsion.

One bite. That was all it would take. He ran his tongue over the part of her throat where her pulse beat the strongest. Things were going too fast. They had done little more than kiss, yet he was already considering penetrating her with his fingers, his cock, and his fangs. Preferably all three simultaneously.

His fingertips brushed coarse hair.

"Marcus, wait," Winifred said.

He immediately withdrew his arm and searched her face for signs of distress. "Did I hurt you?" He hadn't touched a woman so intimately in a very long time. Perhaps he had been too eager with his affection.

"No," she said. "It is only that..." She closed her eyes. "My courses have arrived. So you might not wish to continue."

A wave of heat rippled through his body. He lifted her skirts, ducked beneath, and breathed in a familiar metallic scent. His mouth watered. He spread her thighs apart with shaking hands, then moved a napkin attached to a belt out of his way. Fate had handed him a gift. There was no reason to resist. The offering was already seeping from her body like sap from a tree. All he had to do was lean forward and lap it up.

He brought his nose to her quim and inhaled. The musky scent of her arousal combined with the rich fragrance of blood made his cock spring to attention. There was nothing more appetizing than a woman's monthlies. To a vampire, such a banquet was akin to a sugary treat—luxuriously decadent but lacking nutritional value. He could fill his stomach and be still famished an hour later.

He didn't care.

"I want to continue," he said. "Are you ready?"

She squeezed her thighs around his head. "Yes."

He gently parted her curls with his tongue. The moment he came in contact with her essence, he moaned. It was even better than he remembered. He rasped every surface of her inner lips like a starving man licking his plate after finishing a meal. When there was nothing left, he spread her apart with his thumbs and channeled his blood to form a long, straw-like tongue that he slithered through the tightness of her sheath. He worried at first that it might cause her discomfort, but the way she writhed and pressed herself into his mouth chased those concerns away. He sucked until there was nothing left, then recalled his blood and focused his attention on her clitoris.

She grasped his shoulders. "Oh!"

Her rapid pulse and soft gasps told him she was close. He continued at the same pace and pressure until she came apart, then slowed until she stopped shuddering.

"That was... marvelous," she whispered as he exited her skirts.

He pressed a firm kiss to her cheek. "That is only the start. There is much more for you to learn."

And he couldn't wait to teach her.

Chapter Twenty-Two

"H E WON'T MIND," Winifred said as she stood outside her husband's bedchamber with her fist hovering in the air. After reluctantly leaving Marcus to rest the previous night, she'd returned several times but couldn't seem to gather the courage to knock. Which was absurd, given he'd clearly expressed a desire for them to continue what they'd started.

She closed her eyes and rested her forehead on his door. She was eager to resume their activities, but more than that, she wanted his company. The castle was lonelier than she'd realized, and Marcus slept at the most unusual times. She had been married for mere weeks, but the life she'd imagined after she'd accepted his proposal had been nothing like reality.

Her research would have to be enough. She turned around and walked back to the library. When she arrived and sat down at the same table as she had the previous afternoon, there was an envelope waiting atop the stack of books. She squealed as she tore it open.

Dearest Winifred,

Anastasia delivered your most clever letter. Please understand how much I regret not standing up on your behalf, although I am glad to hear you are getting along well with the earl. When I come of age, it would be my pleasure to become your companion.

As to news, there is not much to tell. Our uncle is eager to see me wed, but I have yet to find a man who I feel would make an appropri-

ate husband. Most of the men Uncle Ethan introduces are terrible bores.

Please write again soon so that I know you received this.

Sincerely,
Felicity

Winifred felt a combination of bubbling happiness for her friend's success and a churning in her gut for Felicity's difficulty with their uncle. Uncle Ethan obviously wanted his ward married and out of his house. If that happened, Winifred wasn't sure if it would be easier or harder to contact her cousin.

She grabbed a sheet of paper and began compiling her response, in which she mentioned her new avenue of occult research. That would be sure to excite Felicity. She finished her letter, sealed it, then gave it to a maid. When the young maid had vanished with her letter and a promise to have it mailed as soon as possible, Winifred leaned back in her chair and looked out the window.

The sun was not quite below the horizon. According to Marcus's nocturnal schedule that she was still not accustomed to, he would be awakening soon, and she had many things she wanted to discuss. She could have waited for him to find her, but she was too restless to sit back and watch the minute hand on the clock on her mantel tick past. She rose out of her chair and walked as quickly as she could into the hallway and then to his room, even though she internally quaked.

When she'd reached his door and knocked, it creaked open.

That was odd. She gently touched her fingers to the wood and pushed.

The room was dark, and there was a sound of shuffling sheets and moaning.

"Marcus?" she whispered.

No response.

She stepped forward, arms outstretched to keep from bumping into anything. As her eyes adjusted to the darkness, she made out a desk and a four-poster bed with the curtains drawn shut.

She should have turned and left, but the soft sound coming from the bed drew her forward, until she stood with one hand clasping the edge of a curtain. Then she peeked inside, and what she saw sent a throb of heat through her.

Marcus was lying on his back, wearing only a nightshirt and a strip of fabric around his eyes like a blindfold. Her gaze traveled down his wide shoulders and chest to his slim waist and his hand clasped tightly around his engorged cock. He lifted his hips as he worked himself. His face was flushed and there were beads of moisture on his forehead. She could not look away, even as her spectacles fogged.

"Marcus," she finally whispered.

His body spasmed, and a milky substance spurted from his cock and dripped down his knuckles. He snatched the blindfold away, grabbed a sheet from where it was bunched by his hips, and flung it over his body.

"Winifred," he said in a voice so husky, it made the skin of her arms erupt into gooseflesh. "Is something wrong?"

She clutched the edge of the curtain. It was impossible not to look at him. His body was lean and muscular, completely different from hers, with fine, black hair covering his shockingly pale abdomen.

"I... I..." She'd seen the nude male form in the books she'd kept hidden deep within her parents' library, but those sketches were in black and white and entirely clinical. "I apologize. I shouldn't have entered without permission."

"You are always welcome." He patted the mattress. "Sit."

She shifted her skirts and carefully perched on the edge of his bed, fully aware that there were only a few layers of fabric between them. She covered her face with her hands. Admitting her desire was tremendously embarrassing.

He wrapped an arm around her shoulders. "Tell me."

She leaned against him and said, all in a rush, "I want to continue where we left off last night."

"Are you certain?"

"Yes." She slid her hand to his bare thigh. "May I touch you?"

He whisked the sheet away faster than she'd thought possible.

Chapter Twenty-Three

MARCUS'S COCK TWITCHED as Winifred circled her index finger and thumb around it, the tips barely meeting. It was the gentlest of touches, a not-so-innocent exploration that made him throw back his head and moan.

"You *do* like that," she said in a teasing voice that did not bode well for him.

"Minx," he said before clasping her about the waist and placing her on his lap. It was both better and worse. Better because the most sensitive area of his body was tucked beneath her skirts. Worse, because it put the most tantalizing area of *her* body out of reach.

"Why did you stop me?" she asked.

Rather than answer, he kissed her until she'd relaxed in his grip and made soft whimpering sounds against his mouth. Only then did he draw back, turn her around, and untie the laces of her gown. Other men might have found the task tedious, but for him it was like unwrapping a present he'd anticipated opening for weeks. With each layer removed, more of her luscious curves were revealed. First her outer gown, which gave him a better look at her gently sloping shoulders. Then her corset cover and petticoats that sparked as he tugged them off and nearly unseated her spectacles, a small price to pay for the way she giggled and squirmed as the fabric lifted over her head. Finally, he tossed her crinoline aside, leaving her perched atop him, wearing only her underthings.

"You are so beautiful," he said as he ran his hands down her sides and cupped her lovely rear.

"Ah!" she flinched. "That's cold."

He chuckled. Her warm skin was scalding against his unnaturally cold flesh, but he welcomed the pain as evidence that he wasn't dreaming.

She grasped the bottom edges of her corset and pressed them together until the metal clasps lifted. The stiffened fabric parted from her bodice, freeing her breasts. He took them in his hands and slid his thumbs over her erect nipples.

"God, Winifred."

She gathered the hem of her shift and pulled it over her head.

He gasped. Imprinted beneath her collarbone was a section of burned flesh in the shape of a sun. He caressed it with his fingers. The symbol was familiar, but he couldn't remember where he'd seen it before. "Who did this to you?"

She sighed. "My uncle. Years ago. As part of a barbaric family tradition." She put her hand over his. "You can touch. It doesn't hurt."

"Was the man who did this at the wedding?"

She touched the scar. "Yes."

He growled. "If I had known, he wouldn't have left this castle alive."

She twisted her lips. "I almost wish you had killed him." Then she shifted out of his grip to stand awkwardly on the bed. She untied her drawers and the belt that held her napkin, then let them pool around her ankles.

His heart leaped into his throat. If he'd thought she was beautiful before, now she was radiant. Every part of her was perfect, from the softness of her stomach to the dips of her thighs and the dark thatch covering her *mons pubis*. He wished he could memorize every curve and wrinkle.

She dug her fingers into her hair and removed a pin. A length of hair unfurled over her shoulders.

His cock ached, but he steadfastly refused to touch it. There was no reason for him to have any further pleasure, beyond what she wished to give him. He shifted his legs to lie on the bed to better enjoy her performance.

She kicked off her slippers, then removed many more pins. They landed with a skittering sound on the floor until her hair formed a cloak around her shoulders. Then she crawled until she was perched above his prone body, her dark hair tickling his skin.

"Touch me," she said. "Bring me pleasure."

It was a command he could not disobey. With one swift movement, he flipped them over and lifted her head to his pillows. With her nude body on full display, she reminded him of paintings of Greek goddesses clothed only in their hair, prepared for worship.

And worship he would.

He allowed himself one touch of her soft breasts before her lack of reaction confirmed what she'd said about having no feeling in that area. He shuffled down, tasting every inch of skin until he reached the thatch of curls that covered the part of her he ached for most. Instead of touching her there, he peeled the stocking from her right leg, then gently grasped her big toe in his teeth.

She let out a sharp cry.

He cupped her foot and spread his thumbs in a massaging motion.

She bucked her hips. "Marcus!"

Quite interesting. He could not remember the last time he'd taken a woman to his bed who had such sensitive feet. It was a welcome surprise, as that body part had always held a particular appeal for him. He eagerly took each of her toes in his mouth while easing the stiff muscles in her shins with his hands. With each passing minute, her breathing grew harsher, and her head thrashed on his pillows.

When he judged her prepared for what was to come next, he returned his attention to her quim and pressed two fingers gently between her damp folds.

She thrust her hips toward his mouth.

He held her down and rasped her with the flag of his tongue.

"Marcus, please!"

He touched one finger to her entrance, then gently eased inside. She was so tight that it took several minutes of stimulating her clitoris before she relaxed enough that he could add a second finger.

She whimpered.

"I know, dearest," he said. "I promise the pain will not last long."

Especially as there was something he could do that a human man could not. He carefully added a third finger, stretching her as gently as possible. Then he withdrew his fangs and pressed the sharp tip of one against her clitoris, just enough to draw a single bead of blood. His jaw ached, but he turned his cheek and let the liquid drip down to the mattress as she shuddered and moaned. The heady scent of her orgasm and the sight of her splayed on his sheets, chest heaving, cheeks flushed, still dripping from where he'd pressed inside her, was too much to bear.

He clasped his cock and stroked himself twice. That was all it took for him to come apart, and in that moment of absolute pleasure, he remembered where he'd seen the symbol burned into her flesh before. It was the sign that had been carved into the side of the village tavern and the emblem of what had once been the most powerful hunter family in Europe.

A family tradition, she'd said. If that was true, then it meant only one thing.

Winifred was a vampire hunter.

Chapter Twenty-Four

WINIFRED ALL BUT skipped down the hall, her cheeks aching from grinning. Marcus was everything she'd ever desired in a husband; intelligent, kind, and attentive to her needs. As it turned out, she had many needs. Her appetite in one area was voracious, but he had proven more than capable of satisfying it. After their vigorous activity, she felt as if she had been using muscles she didn't know she possessed. They had yet to truly consummate their union, but that milestone seemed within reach. She wasn't sure why that one act mattered so much, but Marcus's reluctance made her oddly determined.

When she arrived at the library, she picked up the first of the books her husband had once again left on her table. To no surprise, it was another occult manuscript. She'd meant to ask him about his choice of material, but every time they were alone, she found herself consumed by other matters.

She opened the book. The first chapter gave a history of vampirism as far as the author was aware, starting in the sixteenth century. It also included what amounted to a vampire family tree, with many branching paths. The most prolific of the vampires described had made more than a hundred *fledglings*, as the book called them. The author did not elaborate on how these vampires were born but alluded to a sharing of blood. She jotted that down for a topic of future research. The people listed, she guessed, were like suspected witches in Salem. Poor souls who'd been persecuted likely for matters beyond their control. If Marcus had been alive and suffering his attacks during the same era, he would likely have been branded a witch or a vampire, too.

She found it tremendously ironic that her species had invented monstrous creatures to explain things they did not understand when it was humanity that possessed unfathomable depths of cruelty. Vampires might drink the blood of innocents, but she'd yet to find stories of any who'd branded children the way her uncle had.

She flipped the pages until one name caught her attention.
Lucius Sorrow.
Her maternal great-grandfather.

A distant whine, like a kettle, drowned out the crackling of the fire. She might have dismissed it as a coincidence except for the small symbol of a sun next to his name.

She rubbed her sore neck with one hand. There was no reason to be alarmed. Seeing one of her ancestors in an ancient text meant nothing. Then she noticed the writing at the top of the page and stiffened. She'd apparently passed the chapter on suspected vampires and moved onto something quite different: *vampire hunters*. If she was reading correctly, Lucius Sorrow was credited with taking dozens of lives.

But that was impossible. The stories her mother had told her as a young girl were just that—*stories*.

She slammed the book shut as if it had bitten her and shoved it aside. After the night her uncle had burned the sun into her and Felicity's flesh, she had turned her back on her family lore. The manuscript in front of her had to be a forgery because the only other possibility was that the tales she had been told as a girl were true and she was the product of a line of murderers that went back centuries. She closed her eyes but could not chase the memory of the pages from her mind. Hundreds, if not thousands, of innocent people slaughtered because of a misguided belief in creatures that did not exist.

She wandered out of the library in a haze and returned to her room. When she arrived, there was a letter waiting. The exact distraction she required. She snatched it and cracked the seal.

Winifred,

> *I must see you at once. As I am uncertain if this letter will be in-tercepted, I cannot say more, but please understand that I would not ask you to do this if it were not urgent.*
>
> *Our uncle is accompanying me to the Glasgow museum, where several Sorrow family artifacts are to be placed on display in a tempo-rary exhibit. Please write back as soon as you can and let me know if you could join me for a few days. I am certain we can create a suffi-cient distraction to keep him away for a few hours. We will be staying at the following hotel...*

The tone of the letter was alarming. Winifred found a blank sheet of paper and composed a response that she would, of course, meet her cousin at the specified hotel. She would have to broach the subject with Marcus, given that he couldn't join her on the journey, but surely, he wouldn't refuse her request. When she finished the letter, she sealed it and set it aside. Even if it didn't reach Felicity in time, she knew her cousin would assume she would join her by any means necessary.

The knowledge that she would soon see Felicity again lifted her spirits. They had so much to talk about. She stood from her desk and busied herself with rifling through her wardrobe to select outfits for her trip. It was the job of her lady's maid, but she didn't care. Anything was better than thinking about that manuscript and what it meant that Marcus had left it for her.

Had he wanted her to see Lucius's name?

She would not be staying in Glasgow long, but her red cordu-roy walking suit would be perfect for the crowded city streets.

Maybe Marcus had known her family's shameful history all along, and this was his way of telling her.

Her silver, velvet dress was tempting, but the weather was too warm, and it was unlikely she would have the opportunity to attend social events. She heaved it out of the closet, anyway, and was in the process of shoving it in a trunk when she heard a knock.

"Come in," she said, without looking up.

The door creaked open, and Winifred heard a soft gasp. "My lady, you must allow me to do that!"

Winifred looked down at the half-full trunk and straightened. Keenan was correct. She'd become so desperate to forget what she'd seen that she'd engrossed herself in the task as a distraction.

Keenan bustled over to the wardrobe as Winifred perched on the chair in front of her dressing mirror.

"Do you ken which activities you might partake in?" Keenan asked as she folded a blue silk day dress.

"I will not be staying in Glasgow long. Perhaps a day or two."

Her new marriage was too important to remain away for much longer. She'd left Toronto prepared to accept a life focused on scientific and academic pursuit. Instead, she'd found a relationship that was more fulfilling than publishing any number of papers.

Keenan pulled open a thin drawer, selected several pairs of gloves, and tucked them into the trunk. "Will my lord be joining you?"

Winifred straightened. Keenan's careful tone suggested there was more to the question than initially appeared. Every servant Marcus employed knew he'd remained trapped inside its walls for a decade.

"The earl will remain here," Winifred said.

Keenan did not reply but uttered a soft sigh. That was not a surprise. In the short time she'd spent at the castle, she had quickly realized how much the staff were concerned about their master. She could not blame them. It was not healthy for anyone to spend so much time alone.

She fiddled with the fabric of her dress. She had been raised to believe that a lady did not converse with their servants about casual matters, but talking pushed back her growing unease that there was something very important she was forgetting. "What was the earl like before I arrived?"

Keenan was quiet for several seconds before she lifted her

chin and met Winifred's gaze. "We were quite anxious, if I am honest, my lady."

"How long have you worked here?" Winifred asked. Now that she had started the line of questions, she felt compelled to continue. Other than the few stories he'd told through their letters, she knew so little about him.

"Four years, my lady," Keenan said. "I was a housemaid prior to your arrival."

Winifred turned to the window. The last rays of sunlight had turned the sky into a lovely canvas of pinks and blues. Marcus would soon awaken, and she needed to tell him about Glasgow. She left Keenan to pack and made her way through the halls to his room until her feet suddenly stopped in the same place she'd seen Marcus embracing his valet. Her husband had claimed Smith had been helping him recover from weakness, but her memory supplied something different, an image of Marcus with protruding fangs and a blood-stained mouth.

No. That was impossible. Despite her parents' stories, vampires were nothing more than a folktale spread by superstitious villagers who interpreted anomalies in the natural world by inventing impossible creatures. Even her occult-obsessed cousin would likely find the idea of Marcus being a vampire preposterous.

But the more she resisted the idea, the more she remembered things she'd tried to forget.

Her uncle showing her how to sharpen a wooden stake. Marcus cringing away from a beam of sunlight. Felicity whispering warnings on the day of the wedding. Vincent Sorrow sneering as he'd called Marcus a "monster." Her husband moaning as he'd licked blood from her cut and from between her legs. The way his eyes had glowed bright blue as he'd bared his fangs from behind Smith.

Oh, God. She'd known at some level for days but had refused to acknowledge it. The tales her mother had told her were true. Vampires were real, and her husband was one of them. She'd taken his kindness as evidence that he differed from the men she'd considered as potential husbands in Toronto, but this difference was far worse than she'd imagined.

"So, you figured it out."

Winifred stumbled back against a wall, but it was only Marcus's brother Cordon leaning against the wall with his arms crossed. The tightness of his features and his posture were so familiar that she was overwhelmed with the sense she'd lived this moment before. Then she realized she had. After she'd seen Marcus with Smith and collapsed, she'd found him outside her room, looking precisely as stern as he did now.

He held out an envelope.

She accepted it. "Is this…?"

"The letter I took from you?" His lips quirked. "Yes."

Her pulse pounded in her head as she tore it open.

Winifred,

I can only express my most sincere apology and assure you that no harm will come to you while you remain in this castle. Nor is my valet injured, and he has assured me he is prepared to speak to you to confirm that fact.

You deserve the truth. I have lied to you, my dearest. My human life ended many years ago. What remains in this body is a creature of darkness.

Her knees buckled. She thumped to the floor and touched her chest, where the burn rested beneath all those layers of fabric. Even though she had rejected her ancestors, they remained with her, their blood pumping through her body, as unchangeable as the mark emblazoned on her skin.

Marcus was a vampire, and she was a descendent of vampire hunters. Her uncle had only claimed there was a feud between their families because he'd known she would not have believed the truth.

A hysterical giggle traveled up her throat. No wonder her uncle had been furious at her marriage. They were like Romeo and Juliet, although she hoped their fates weren't heading in the same direction as Shakespeare's lovers.

Lucius Sorrow had killed dozens of vampires. How many had her uncle killed? Did Felicity know? Was that why she'd acted so strangely before their uncle had taken her away?

Winifred leaned so that her head rested against the cold, stone wall. Dwelling on what might happen next would not help her. If she was to become a scholar, she must approach this new information rationally.

If vampires were real, then they must be a different species. Perhaps, like Darwin's finches, humans had evolved to adapt to different environments. The pounding in her head faded. Yes, that was much better. Thinking of Marcus in scientific terms took him out of the realm of mythology and into something much more logical. After all, society often feared that which it could not adequately explain, and there were still things being discussed regarding electricity that defied explanation. She cracked her stiff shoulders and returned to the letter.

> *What I have not lied about is how much I care about you. From the moment I received your first letter, I felt a strong connection between us. That is the reason I now write. If what you now know about me means you can no longer abide my presence, then I will do as I have done several times in my long existence and arrange my own "death." The title, granted to me by Queen Victoria, will pass to one of my siblings, but you will have a generous widow's portion. You will be free to do as you wish and shall have the means to support yourself for the rest of your life.*

Her eyes burned. The words could not have been penned by a monster. She could practically feel the sadness radiating from the page. She skimmed through the last of what he'd written before she lost her courage.

> *But if you choose to stay, I will agree to any terms you set. Consider, for example, that the journals I provided were not written by my grandfather, but are my own words, and there are many more. You may have them all, and as much of my time as you wish to devote to research.*

Do not fear me, Winifred. I would gouge out my heart before I would allow any harm to come to you.

Yours,
Marcus

The tears she'd successfully forced back dripped down her cheeks. The emotion in his writing tugged at her heart, even as she acknowledged the bait he'd set on the hook. If she understood him correctly, Marcus had lived for hundreds of years. That meant he possessed *firsthand knowledge* of significant historical events and might share that knowledge with her. It was an opportunity that would have made any scholar salivate, and she was no exception.

All she had to do was continue to live with a vampire.

Chapter Twenty-Five

MARCUS WAS SITTING on his bed, pressing a piece of clean cloth against an oozing sore on his shoulder and considering what to do about the fact that his wife probably wanted to kill him, when Cordon burst through the door, nearly sending it flying off its hinges.

"Brother, you must—" Cordon said before his expression twisted in horror.

Marcus removed the cloth from his skin with a wince. "So. Now you know." He hadn't wanted his brother to discover his worsening condition, but it was too late. The symptoms that had abated after consuming Winifred's and Smith's blood had returned. He'd allowed himself to be careless, setting aside his experiments in favor of Winifred's well-meaning but pointless exercises in stoicism. Now there was no doubt.

He was dying.

"How long have you been hiding this?" Cordon asked.

Marcus buttoned his shirt. "It doesn't matter." His suffering would soon be over. Anything that followed was none of his concern.

Cordon crossed the room in a flash. He grasped Marcus's shoulders and shook. "Don't you dare give up."

Marcus felt hot and cold at the same time. This was exactly why he'd kept the secret. He maneuvered out of his brother's grasp. "What did you come here to tell me?"

Cordon scowled. "You haven't changed." His irises glowed

blue. "When will you stop pretending to be like Marguerite? You'll never be able to replace her."

Ice formed around Marcus's heart. He'd given his brother more than enough chances. His continued disrespect was unacceptable. He rose to his feet, withdrew his fangs, then lunged, fully intending to force the younger vampire to his knees. Instead, Cordon caught him about the waist and slammed him to the floor. Marcus channeled his blood into his shoulders until a fierce pain bloomed in his head and made him cry out.

"Stop, brother," Cordon whispered. "Please. You cannot beat me."

Marcus gritted his teeth and bared his neck. Only then did Cordon release him. Marcus curled into a ball, unwilling to see the disgust on his brother's face. The façade was over. He had lost his authority, and it was only a matter of time before his family imploded and his siblings killed each other or were absorbed into other nests.

"Helena searched the archives," Cordon said. "You were right. There is a line of hunters associated with the sun symbol. We tracked them through Lucius Sorrow to a family of at least thirty. Brother, you should know that the countess—"

"Is one of them." Marcus crawled back to his bed and pulled himself into a sitting position. "I know."

He assumed her family had carefully inserted her into his life as a distraction while they poisoned his animals and slaughtered the birds in his aviary. The only thing he didn't understand was why her family hadn't simply killed him. They'd had plenty of chances.

Perhaps they wanted him to suffer first.

"She's not a hunter," Cordon said.

Marcus stared at his brother. "What?"

Cordon scratched the back of his neck. "She never completed her training. From what I discovered, there was a violent argument between Mrs. Belltree and her brother. A few weeks later, the Belltrees fled to Toronto. The countess was only a girl when it happened." He sighed. "I owe you an apology, brother. Whatever else has occurred, your wife is innocent."

Marcus felt as if an enormous weight had been lifted off his shoulders.

Cordon shifted. "However, I *might* have given her your letter."

As if she'd been waiting for a cue, there was a loud knock on his door.

"Come in." Marcus said, while glaring at his brother.

Winifred entered, looking as pale as the afternoon her family had left. She met his gaze and pressed her lips together, but before she could say anything, she glanced at Cordon and straightened.

"Good evening," Cordon said. "Do not let me interrupt." He stuck his hands in his pockets and walked around Winifred. When he left, she furrowed her brow. "He's a vampire too, isn't he?" She shook her head. "I feel as though I've taken leave of my senses."

"You haven't."

She gave him a penetrating stare, then rushed forward and put her face close to his.

"W-What are you doing?" he asked.

She narrowed her eyes. "Turn them blue."

"Pardon?"

She put her index fingers and thumbs on his forehead and cheeks, then pulled his eyelids open. "Make your irises glow. You did it when you bit Smith. I want to see it for myself and confirm it's not a trick."

He clenched his fingers on the leather arms of his chair so hard, he feared he would have to send it for repair after this interlude. But he would do whatever she asked against the slim chance she chose to stay. He focused on her neck, on the faint vein beneath the surface.

His fangs descended.

"Fascinating," Winifred said. She released her grip on his face, then lifted his upper lip with her thumb. He obligingly opened his mouth so she could inspect his teeth. She slid the pad of her index finger down a fang and was about to move it over the sharp tip when he grasped her hand and jerked it away.

She leaned back. "Why did you do that?"

"You would have cut yourself and I-I do not want to taste your blood."

"I see." She walked over to sit in the chair opposite him and perched on it. "So, that much is true. You consume blood. Interesting. How often do you need it? Does it have to be human?"

So, it was to be an interrogation. That, at least, was easier than restraining himself while she poked at his face. Her reaction was much more rational than he'd expected. Perhaps her hunter family had taught her something, after all. He could have told her he knew about her lineage, but it would be more revealing to see how—if—she brought up the subject herself.

"Several times a day," he finally said. "Animal blood is my usual fare, as you might have guessed from the number of livestock the estate maintains."

Her fingers twitched. She patted her sides, then twisted her lips. "I wish I could take notes."

He could not help but laugh. "There is no need. If you want to know more about my kind, I can tell you anything you wish. There are also many more texts you could read." His lips quirked. "Although you would not find them in the library."

"Books," she repeated. "Like the ones you left me to read. That's why you didn't tell me. You wanted me to figure it out myself."

"Yes. Then you saw me with Smith and even though you didn't remember, I knew you would eventually."

She curled her arms around her knees. "What really happened with Smith? Was he one of your victims?"

He winced. His nest siblings preferred "donor" to "victim," but they usually drank from their lovers. Marcus, stuck in his castle, had not had that option before now. "No. Smith is the first human I've bitten in centuries. Mrs. Gillanders, Gillanders, and Smith are the only members of my staff who know what I am."

She furrowed her brow. "Then why…?"

This was the part of the explanation he hadn't been looking forward to. "Smith volunteered." When she didn't respond, he reluctantly continued. "He knew of my weakened state and did not want me to assault a servant. Inadvertently." He held up his hands. "I would never intentionally harm an innocent, but I was not entirely in control of myself."

She paled. "What do you mean?"

"I had gone too long without human blood." He covered his face with his hands. "God, Winifred. I am a monster."

"I would not say that."

He peered through his fingers. "You wouldn't?"

"I think what you did was quite considerate."

He lowered his hands. "Considerate" was not a word he had applied to himself in a very long time. Callous, careless, complacent, but not *considerate*. She continued to surprise him.

"Yes," she said firmly. "If I understand correctly, you did nothing wrong. Your valet made an offer, and you accepted. What I witnessed was nothing more than a consensual exchange." Her eyes lidded. "This bite of yours. Does it hurt?"

He chuckled. "Yes, but it is also quite pleasurable." He lowered his voice, although there was unlikely to be anyone else listening. "You've felt the touch of my fangs once already."

She raised her right hand. "Our wedding night."

"Yes, and when we…" He gestured to her skirts.

Her cheeks turned bright red and her spectacles fogged.

He put his hand over his heart. "You have my word that I will not do it again."

She stared at her palm for several seconds before dropping it to his lap. "What if I *asked* you to bite me?"

He dug his fingers into the arms of his chair to stop himself from reaching for her. "Absolutely not."

THE VEHEMENCE OF Marcus's refusal made Winifred stand and put her hands on her hips. "What is wrong with my blood?"

His nostrils flared. "Do not make this about you."

She wasn't sure why his rejection bothered her. Perhaps because now that she knew that his bite was pleasurable, every time she closed her eyes, she saw him with his arms around his valet. Or because knowing he wasn't human made it impossible to rid herself of an insidious thought that she would never be enough for him. He'd lived for *centuries*. Compared to that, she might well have been an entertaining plaything to use until she grew too old or frail to be of value.

There was one other possibility. She could be displacing her shock and fear from learning vampires were real into an emotion that was easier to process. Unfortunately, while it was relatively easy to analyze her own mental state with cool detachment, it was significantly more difficult to change her behavior. The rational part of her was willing to make observations, but it would not take away the pain in her heart.

Maybe seducing Marcus would.

She crossed the room and crouched so that their heads were at the same level, then pressed her lips against his. Two slight lumps confirmed his fangs were still out, but he kept his mouth firmly shut. She tried again, kissing him with more force. He moaned deep in his throat.

"Choose me," she whispered. "Let me give you what you need." Then the image that was seared on the inside of her eyelids would vanish, and the churning in her gut when she imagined Marcus remaining the same while she aged and eventually died would stop.

"You don't understand," Marcus said in a tight voice. "Drinking from Smith was a last resort. I could have killed him." He tilted his head and rested it on her shoulder. "Your blood is unlike anything I've ever tasted. It is too dangerous."

She wrapped her arms around his shoulders. "Then make me yours. Consummate our union."

It wouldn't get rid of the nefarious voice in her head that insisted a vampire could never truly be with a human, but it might silence it for a while until she had time to examine her options.

Marcus hefted her in his arms and carried her to his bed. First came her bodice, lifted over her head. Then her corset, skirt, petticoats, and hoopskirt. Finally, he crouched and made her place one hand on his shoulder while he removed her slippers, then rolled down her stockings.

"Your feet are lovely," he said. "Do you ever apply balm?" He nibbled her heel. "Your toes would look delectable slathered in oil. I could do it for you."

She was too lost in the pleasurable feeling of his hands massaging her shins to answer. Being so exposed while he remained fully clothed made her feel like he could shatter her with a glance. She touched the top button of his shirt.

"No," he said before placing her knees on his shoulders.

She pursed her lips. "I want to see you."

"Next time," he said. Then he ran his fangs along her inner thigh, and it no longer mattered. The conflagration he'd sparked in her abdomen threatened to consume her.

"Do you know what I felt when you pressed your lips to Smith's throat?" she asked. "Envy. I was jealous you'd picked him over me. I feel it even more now that he has given you something you won't accept from me." She curled her fingers in his hair. "Stop holding back. I don't want to be worshipped. I want *you*. All of you."

Perhaps more than that, she wanted things to go back to normal. She didn't want to fear her own husband, but until he released his tightly held restraints, she'd never know how much he was keeping from her.

"I'm terrified of hurting you," Marcus said. He kissed each of her toes. "I'm afraid that if you see the real me, you'll understand how evil I truly am and you'll run away the first chance you get."

"I won't," she whispered. Despite her tumultuous emotions, she felt the same way now as she had when she'd arrived. There was nothing to fear in the dark. True monsters, like her uncle, did not need to hide themselves. They were comfortable in the light because they knew they'd always be safe from the consequences of their actions. It was Marcus's very reluctance to reveal his nature that confirmed she'd been right about him all along.

He might have been a vampire, but he was no monster.

Chapter Twenty-Six

"I WISH YOU could see yourself the way I see you," Winifred said, in a voice so soft it made Marcus's heart leap into his throat.

He brushed strands of hair over her shoulder. "I could not bear it if I broke you."

Hundreds of humans had died by his hand before he'd developed the control necessary to push back his vampiric nature. It had been nearly two centuries since he'd accidentally taken a mortal life during a feeding, but he dared not bite her while there remained even a miniscule risk.

She screwed up her nose. "I am not a piece of pottery, Marcus."

He gathered her against his chest. "You do not understand. You are"—he grasped for the correct words—"the light that has brightened the dark confines of this castle." She was more than that, of course. She was his rescuer, perfection personified.

"I need you," Winifred whispered.

He exhaled a shaky breath as he unbuttoned the fall of his trousers and released his cock. What he was considering doing was dangerous, given how tenuous his control had been as of late, but he'd told her the truth. He burned for her with a fury that was beyond his ability to ignore. He grabbed a pillow, lifted her hips to place it beneath her, then brought the head of his cock to her quim.

She ran her fingers down her abdomen. "W-Will it fit?"

"It will." He pressed a kiss to the scar between her breasts. "We don't have to do this. There are other ways… ways that would be better for you." It would take everything in him to stop, but her comfort and safety were his only concern.

She clenched her fingers in his shirt. "No. I've waited long enough. Make me your wife."

Her determination filled him with a fluttering warmth, even as the slight movement of the fabric draped over his bruised flesh made him wince. He ignored the pain and rubbed his shaft through her folds, coating himself in her essence and giving her ample opportunity to change her mind. When she relaxed, he grasped her hip in one hand and entered her.

She gasped, but he was used to her reaction to his coldness. As expected, she soon relaxed and tilted her head back.

He had only penetrated her an inch, but he already trembled with restraint. He wouldn't be able to last long, but this moment, her first experience, had to be as perfect as he could make it, given the circumstances.

She took him easily until her curls were pressed against his. He savored each twitch of her sheath. The urge to move was overwhelming, but he held himself in place until she stopped squirming.

"What next?" she asked, between panting breaths.

He drew back until he nearly fell out of her, then eased back in. The scorching heat of her quim clasped around him was almost too much to bear.

"Again," she demanded.

He did as she'd asked, while also forming a protrusion out of the base of his cock with his blood. With each thrust, it rubbed against her clitoris and vibrated. There were other things he could do to enhance her pleasure, but she was already so close that he would save them for another time.

Then his rhythm faltered, and he felt her slip away from the edge. He grunted in frustration and tried to slow down, but he was too close to his own limit. Unable to resist, he withdrew his fangs, leaned down, and brushed the gentlest of scratches along her collarbone. A bead of blood formed and dripped down her pale skin. As she cried out and spasmed around his cock, his resistance shattered. He leaned forward and licked the blood away. The moment it touched his tongue, he came apart so powerfully that he saw spots.

When he could think again, he curled onto his side and drew her back against his chest. "That was…extraordinary."

She placed her hand atop his. "For me as well, but…" She twisted around until they were face to face. "Why did you apologize?"

He ran his fingertips along a faint, white mark on her collarbone. "I vowed I would not taste your blood again, but I couldn't stop myself. At least it was only a drop."

Such a small amount, yet it had chased away the minor aches that had plagued him since he'd awoken that evening. He felt even stronger than he had after Smith's donation, all thanks to her.

She sniffed. "You could have taken more."

That statement made his stomach twist into knots, so instead of responding, he tugged her so her cheek was against his chest. He still could not believe she was in his bed and had allowed him to taste her mouth, her flesh, her blood. She was everything he'd dreamed of and more.

He wished he could be the same for her. She was not a beautiful creature to be caged so he alone could admire her plumage and her song. She deserved excitement. Novelty. The company of people who would appreciate her passion for history.

All things he could not give to her in his current state.

He draped an arm over his eyes. Mere hours ago, he had accepted that his life was nearly over. Now, he could not bear the thought of leaving Winifred. What he felt for her was so far beyond the mere concept of "love" that it was laughable. According to Cordon, if she were his mate, they would have bonded already.

Unless she did not feel the same way.

He dismissed the thought. If Winifred did not love him yet, he was certain she would, in time. But if fate were so cruel as to place her in his life but not have her be his fated mate, then he did not want one.

There had to be another way. The scientific world rarely operated in absolutes. All he had to do was identify and extract the component out of human blood that alleviated the symptoms of atrophy. Then he could devote his life to Winifred and forget about the messy complications of mating and telepathic bonds once and for all.

Chapter Twenty-Seven

"MY COUSIN HAS asked me to join her in Glasgow on an urgent matter," Winifred said as she played with the buttons of the shirt Marcus had refused to remove, even as he'd thrust deep inside her. It was a tad disappointing, but she did not have the heart to push him. Given enough time, her persistence would erode the wall he'd erected between them.

"Glasgow," Marcus repeated. "Are you certain this is not a trap?" He propped himself up on his elbow. "They are hunters, and you are the wife of a vampire. They might not hesitate to kill you."

She was shaking her head before he finished. "Not Felicity. Uncle Ethan might have nefarious intentions, but my cousin is innocent." She fought back tears as she tried to find the words that would make him understand. "It doesn't matter, Marcus. Even if it is a trap, I must get Felicity away from our uncle. He *branded* us. I fear what he might do before Felicity comes of age next month."

He tugged a strand of her hair. "You care for her deeply."

She placed her hand over his. "You should come with me. We could cover the windows in the carriage."

"It's not that simple."

She sighed. He was right, of course. It was unreasonable to expect him to progress so quickly from a dinner party to traveling to an entirely different city. "I don't want to leave you alone, but I have no choice. Felicity insisted the matter was urgent, and I cannot ignore the opportunity to wrench her out of my uncle's grasp."

He ran his fingers along her spine. "I could make you stay."

"You wouldn't dare." He was stronger than her, but he slept through the day. "What will you do, lock me in my room? Have a servant follow me while you rest?"

He sighed. "Will you at least allow one of my brothers to accompany you?"

She kissed his cheek. "As long as they follow at a discreet distance. If my family have set a trap, I do not want to alert them before I have spoken to Felicity."

"That will have to do." He grasped her chin, tilted her head up, then kissed the tip of her nose. "But I shall miss you every moment you are gone."

She looped her arms around his neck. "There remains an hour until sunrise." Every second of which she intended to spend in his embrace, clothed or not. Preferably the latter.

He waggled his eyebrows. "I believe my lady requires a bath before her journey." He kissed her once more before pulling the thick, braided rope in the corner of the room.

"Marcus!" She buried herself under the blankets. Inviting his valet into the room while she was unclothed was beyond scandalous.

There was a rap at the door. Marcus turned to her and pressed his index finger to his lips in a shushing gesture. She giggled despite herself, then flipped the blanket over her head and kept as still as possible. It was rather titillating, indulging in activities that would have made her mother drop into a faint.

She heard creaking, followed by murmuring, then a loud thud. She popped her head out of the blanket as Marcus returned, wearing a smile that made the hair on the back of her neck stand up.

"Smith will arrange for a copper tub and buckets of hot water to be brought up," he said. Then he untied the curtains around the bed before crawling in to join her.

The next several minutes were spent trying to keep from making noise as she heard movement. A task that was made much more difficult by Marcus rasping his tongue along the sensitive skin of her inner thighs. She bit the inside of her cheek but could not help the soft sounds that escaped her lips as he slid his fingers in and out of her sheath and swirled his tongue around her clitoris. The pleasure built until it burst, rippling through her in waves. As she savored the last of the gentle pulses, Marcus gathered her in his arms.

"It is time for you to bathe, my lady."

She snickered, then shrieked as he bounded across the room and dumped her into the tub. The water was slightly too hot for her liking, but she welcomed the heat because it made parts of her that had been tense all day relax. She slid down with a satisfied sigh, then looked at her husband with half-lidded eyes. He rolled up his sleeves, bearing his forearms.

She lifted one damp leg. "Are you not joining me?"

He fell to his knees and slid his hands into the water. "It is my duty to bathe you, my lady."

"As you wish," she said. If he wanted to play being a servant, she would not stop him. She tilted her head so the back of her neck rested against the rim as he produced a bar of soap and stroked it down one leg and then the next. The firm movements of his hands chased away what remained of her anxiety from the evening. Then he tucked the bar between her legs and made her squeal.

"*Marcus!*"

The cheek of the man. She tangled her fingers in his cravat. But as she tugged him closer, he flinched.

She shifted onto her knees. "What is it?"

He grabbed a towel and draped it over his neck. "Nothing of importance."

She felt a sinking sensation in her stomach as she remembered how he'd refused to remove his shirt. "Don't lie to me."

"Winifred—"

She grasped both ends of the towel to prevent him from rising. "You *will* show me."

He didn't verbally agree, but the way the lines on his face deepened told her she'd broken the last of his defenses. She released her grip and gestured for him to bring him a robe. When she was warm and dry, she sat on his bed and crossed her arms. "Well?"

He touched his top button. "Before you see this, I want you to understand that there is nothing you could have done. This… was inevitable."

She scowled. That was precisely the disclaimer she would have expected from someone who thought the exact opposite. "Stop stalling and show me."

He did, and it was like someone had punched her in the gut.

"Oh, Marcus…" She touched the red-brown edge of a bruise on his chest. "What happened?"

He clenched his hands at his sides in a way that suggested he was avoiding reaching for something with which to cover himself. It made her heart ache that he felt he had to hide from her.

"I believe it is… an illness," he said, speaking as if every word were being pulled from him by force. "One unique to my species. The attacks were the first stage, and this is the second."

The attacks she'd tried to help him manage. In forcing him to endure practice sessions, she'd interrupted his research. It was her fault his condition had worsened. She knew he hadn't discovered a cure, but perhaps… "Is there anything that improves the symptoms?"

He didn't respond, but his lips thinned. He was keeping things from her again.

"Marcus," she said sharply. "Tell me."

He exhaled harshly. "Every vampire has a mate, one soul in the entire world with whom they are destined to bond. It is the lack of this mating bond that causes the disease mate atrophy. I did not believe it at first, but…" He ran a hand through his hair.

"Earlier this year, Cordon lapsed into a fever and nearly died. His symptoms only abated after he mated with his wife. That was what changed my mind."

It was an incredible story, but she was more interested in what he hadn't said. Each time he spoke, pieces slotted together in her mind, but she could not yet see the complete puzzle. He'd claimed he did not drink from humans, but the way he'd licked her finger the night of their wedding suggested his resistance was not because of any lack of desire. In fact, he'd seemed far more energetic after she'd caught him with Smith.

"Human blood," she said. "That's what heals you. Well, that's easy, then." She tilted her head to the side and let her robe slide open. "Drink from me."

He jerked away from her. "No!"

"Why not?" It wasn't as if this were the first time she'd offered. His continued reluctance to let her give him what he desperately needed was tremendously frustrating.

"You do not know what you are asking," he said.

"I am asking you to let me help you."

He shook his head. "I made a vow not to bite humans, Winifred. A vow I have broken several times since you arrived." He licked his lips. "You don't know h-how many p-people I've killed during feedings." His throat worked. "I could not live with myself if anything happened to you. I would rather die of this affliction."

Her stomach churned. She'd tried very hard not to dwell on the idea of him taking human lives.

But it was not as if he was hunting for sport. He was a predator, and humans were prey. She could not blame a cat for eating a mouse.

"You are trying to be better," she said. "That is what matters."

His expression shuttered. "You don't understand."

There he went, cutting a part of himself off from her again. She was growing rather sick of it.

"Please, Marcus."

His eyes glowed bright blue. "I will not risk forcing you to make the choice I was not given. The answer is no."

A snippet from one of the occult books he'd provided returned to her. *A sharing of blood.* That was how vampires spawned offspring. With that fact, the puzzle came together. He feared if he drank too much, he would feel compelled to turn her into a vampire.

She placed her fingers gently on his chest. "I'm not afraid, Marcus. If the worst happens, I won't blame you."

If there was the smallest chance that biting her would heal him, then she was willing to try. Even if it meant giving up the sun and her mortal life. None of that mattered because Marcus had become her entire world. She could not imagine a future without him. Plus, he'd lived for centuries. As a vampire, she would have ample opportunity to research any subject she wished. She could visit the sights of natural disasters—once Marcus could better manage his attacks. They could live through history together. There was the problem of feeding, but if Marcus had abstained from killing humans for so long, she was certain she could adapt as well. The more she thought about it, the more promising the idea seemed.

Unfortunately, he did not share her enthusiasm.

He stepped back. "Visit Glasgow. Walk beneath the warm rays of the sun and rescue your cousin if you can. But be cautious. It is unlike hunters to allow a vampire to live. When you return, if I have not found a viable treatment, then I will do as you ask."

Once again, it was what he *didn't* say that angered her. He obviously expected that the threat of her returning before he'd succeeded would be sufficient motivation to work through his pain.

She crossed her arms. "I'm not going anywhere. Not if there's a chance I'll return and find you dead. I will send a maid to Glasgow with instructions to escort my cousin back. Felicity's urgent matter will have to wait."

"Winifred, please. I don't want you to walk into a trap, but I cannot—"

"I said no. I am not leaving unless you drink my blood."

He swayed on his feet. "Do you know what happens after a vampire is turned?" His hair seemed to float away from his head. "If the maker is strong, the fledgling might last a few hours before blood lust consumes them. My maker did not stop me. I killed dozens, Winifred, before I came to my senses. Perhaps hundreds. I hated her for it, and for making me into a monster."

She couldn't imagine how awful it had to have been to realize what he'd done, and to feel such anger toward the woman who had turned him. But as much as she understood his logic, she would not accept it.

"It's not the same," she whispered. "I trust you to stop me."

Then his expression shuttered. "I will not risk turning the descendant of a hunter into a vampire."

It felt like he'd plunged a dagger into her heart. "You don't mean that."

When he did not respond, she stumbled backward, then fled the room.

Chapter Twenty-Eight

MARCUS STARED OUT the window, willing Winifred's carriage to reappear. His instincts urged him to find shelter, but he didn't care. The pain of knowing he'd hurt her was worse than the glare of the sun.

Why hadn't he just bitten her?

He closed his eyes. He knew why. If he gave in and drank too much, he would be forced to let her die or turn her. As the former was impossible, the latter meant she might come to hate him as he hated his own maker. There was love in his heart for Marguerite, but it was small compared to his resentment that she'd robbed him of his mortality and allowed him to kill so many innocents. Winifred was upset now, but her anger would fade.

He wrenched himself from the window and reached out with his senses for his brothers. They might not have approved of his marriage, but he hoped he wouldn't have to command them to follow Winifred and guard her against hunter attacks.

"You have really done it this time," Cordon said from behind him.

Marcus sighed and turned to face his siblings.

Cordon wore a silver-and-black plaid suit jacket and matching trousers. The colors and slim fit suited his tall frame looked as if he hadn't rested in days and met Marcus's look with a scowl.

"Winifred has gone to Glasgow," Marcus said. "I want one of you to follow her." The words sounded weak, even to him. He wondered if this was how Cordon had felt when he'd thought he'd been dying. That made Marcus feel even worse about not coming to his brother's side. He truly was a failure as head of the family. Maybe it was time to let someone else take over.

"You allowed her to leave?" Cordon asked. "It could be a trap."

Marcus slouched over his desk and put his head on his folded arms. "What am I to do, brother? Lock her in her room?"

He would not make the castle a prison for her because he knew how it felt to be confined.

Cordon made a rude sound. "You have known this woman for mere months."

Jonathan let out a sharp laugh. "You betray yourself, Cordon. How long after you met Katherine did you marry her?"

Cordon scowled. "It is not the same. Kitty was my mate." His expression softened. "It was love at first bite."

Marcus straightened. "What do you mean?"

"Don't get him started," Jonathan said as he plucked a delicately carved wooden box from Marcus's desk. It was a trinket Marcus had picked up decades before his involuntary confinement. A specific sequence of actions was required to open a secret compartment. Jonathan frowned as he tilted it around.

"Slide the—" Marcus started before Jonathan shushed him. Marcus left his younger brother to his curiosity and looked at Cordon, who was staring out the window with his arms crossed.

"Please, brother," Marcus said. "Tell me what happened between you and Kitty." He wasn't sure why it was so important, but something deep in his chest told him he had to know what his brother had to say.

Cordon rubbed his chin with his thumb and forefinger. "Well, you know that when I met her, I had given up."

"I recall it well," Marcus said. Cordon had created a list of a hundred scandalous activities he'd wanted to complete before he died of mate atrophy. Marcus and Jonathan had scoffed at the idea. It no longer seemed so foolish.

"Kitty was impossible to resist," Cordon said, his tone wistful.

"She later admitted she felt it, too, but refused to acknowledge it." He shook his head with a chuckle. "She willingly gave her body but held her heart back until the very end. Much as I did. But after tasting her, I knew I could have no other. Her blood healed parts of me I hadn't known were broken."

Cordon continued talking, but Marcus was too struck by the comparison between what his brother was describing and his own situation with Winifred. She'd been irresistible and her blood had caused a similar reaction. It was almost the reverse situation, where Winifred had been open with her affection from the day she'd arrived in the castle, but Marcus had kept his distance—or, at least, he'd tried. Staying away from Winifred had been as futile and stopping the sun from rising.

When Cordon stopped speaking, Marcus reluctantly asked the question that had been bouncing around his head for hours, but he'd refused to acknowledge. "You've spoken of it before, but would you remind me again how you formed the mating bond?"

The sound of wood hitting the floor with a thud made both Marcus and Cordon turn. The puzzle box lay discarded on the floor between Jonathan's legs, with the secret compartment open.

Jonathan scowled. "I cannot believe this. Look at what you've done." He picked up one of Marcus's silver flasks. "This is science. *This* is innovation. You are an inventor, brother. If anyone can find a way to avoid mating, it's you. Don't give in to fate."

The back of Marcus's neck burned. Having his younger brother speak to him in such a way made his temper rise, but he tamped it down. Jonathan was only reacting the same way Marcus had when Cordon had presented his list of scandalous tasks he'd intended to complete before he died. Marcus had not believed his brother was dying, at first. It had taken Cordon's miraculous recovery after marrying Kitty to change Marcus's mind.

He staggered over to his chair and fell into it. "I love Winifred. Her blood heals me more effectively than any concoction. She *must* be my fated mate, but we have not bonded. Is there something else I must do?"

Jonathan threw up his hands. "I've had enough. I'll head to Glasgow. Anywhere is better than here." Then he stormed out of the room, letting the door slam behind him. Marcus winced. He would have to mend things with his brother later, but for now, he was more concerned about making sure he had all the information he could gather from Cordon. His brother had told the story of his mating several times, but Marcus had been too focused on finding a scientific alternative to listen.

Cordon walked over to the mantel, removed a cigar from a box sitting there, then lit it in the flames of the hearth. "The bond comes first." He put the cigar to his mouth and puffed, then came to sit across from Marcus. "If she is your mate, then when you are both open to love, the connection will snap into place." He put his index finger and thumb on his temple, then gestured outward. "It was not something we attempted. It simply...happened." He frowned. "I cannot explain it. One moment I was certain I was dying, and the next, Kitty was pressing my mouth to her neck and urging me to drink. It was at that moment that the bond formed." He closed his eyes. "I will never forget the moment her mind first touched mine."

Cordon's blissful expression made Marcus want to strangle him. It wasn't fair that Cordon had found his mate first. Marcus was the eldest. He should have been the one helping his siblings find their mates, not Cordon.

A bitter taste filled his mouth. Being jealous of Cordon was pointless. Marcus had surrendered leadership of the nest when he'd fled to Scotland. He waited for Cordon to open his eyes, then asked, "Was that when the symptoms faded?"

Cordon took another puff. "Not immediately, but yes. Marguerite believed it was the lack of the bond that causes the atrophy."

Marcus tapped his fingers on the arm of his chair. "But you did not need to turn Katherine into a vampire first. The bond formed while she was still human." That meant there might be a way to let Winifred help him without risking her life.

Assuming she hadn't already been captured. Her carriage had left a full quarter hour before Jonathan had followed.

He put his head in his hands. "I never should have let her go. If anything happens to her…" The hunters were merciless. If they decided Winifred was 'tainted' because of her marriage to him, they might treat her like any other vampire they hunted.

"Do not worry, brother," Cordon said. He tapped his temple. "I can speak to my mate through our mental bond even when we are far apart. Kitty is watching your wife even as we speak."

A wave of giddiness passed through Marcus. "Thank God."

He would trust his brothers to protect her, and when she returned, he would tell her exactly how he felt.

Until then, he'd do his best to stay alive.

Chapter Twenty-Nine

W INIFRED PULLED OPEN the curtain in her room on the top floor of the Clarence Hotel and gasped. In the bright light of morning, George Square was beautiful, with four paths in the grassy plaza leading to a statue of a mounted general. Ladies wearing wide-brimmed hats lavishly piled with flowers and feathers promenaded along the sidewalk and the street was busy, with carriage rattling along the cobblestones.

It was such a change from the castle that she stared, open-mouthed, for several seconds before remembering she was supposed to be meeting Felicity for breakfast. Keenan had awakened Winifred an hour earlier, but it had taken ages to sort out what Winifred would wear—a chartreuse twill walking suit— and then Keenan had done up her hair and selected a hat and proper shoes. It had been weeks since she'd last dressed appropriately for her station, during the dinner with the vicar and his wife.

She felt like a soldier wearing a suit of armor, preparing to venture into battle. Or, in her case, a crowded hotel lobby. It was exciting and intimidating, but most of all—lonely. Especially knowing Marcus was back at the castle. She already regretted leaving so abruptly. That he knew about her ancestors didn't matter. He had only spoken to her cruelly because he'd wanted her to give up trying to help him, and she'd foolishly let him.

"Are you ready, my lady?" Keenan asked.

Winifred turned away from the window and joined her lady's maid. "Yes."

Together, they descended to the crowded first floor and made their way to the restaurant.

Felicity was there, sitting at a table in the garden wearing a lovely, yellow cotton day dress with a heart-shaped neckline and a wide, straw hat. She lifted her teacup to her lips in an unhurried manner, nothing like a woman in desperate need of rescue.

Her cousin was well. Winifred had feared she'd find her cousin a babbling mess, but clearly whatever had caused Felicity to write with such urgency was not so important that it couldn't wait until after breakfast. Winifred's legs wobbled before she caught herself and strode forward.

Felicity spotted them through the French doors, straightened, and lifted a hand in welcome. Winifred left Keenan with other servants of guests and joined her cousin at a table in the garden.

"Thank you for coming," Felicity said with a smile. "I do apologize for drawing you away so soon after your wedding."

"What is it, then?" Winifred asked. She lowered her voice. "Do you need my help?"

"Not at the moment."

Winifred's leg bounced beneath the table. She stilled it. "Will you come back to the castle with me?"

Felicity leaned back. "Absolutely not!"

The strength of her cousin's refusal angered Winifred more than if Felicity had outright insulted her husband. "What is it, then? Why did you need me to come?"

Felicity chewed her lower lip. "The earl did not accompany you?"

Winifred sighed. "No. What is wrong, Fel? Are you well?"

Felicity squirmed in her seat. "Yes. Living with Uncle Ethan is challenging, but he last left me alone these past few weeks. I… I wished to see you. That is all. I thought it would be easier for you to travel here than all the way back to London."

Winifred remembered Marcus's warning about a trap. She hadn't thought Felicity capable of such deception. "Uncle Ethan did not warn you against seeing me?"

Felicity laughed. "Of course he did, Winnie. He ordered me to remain in my room while he dealt with some business this morning." She scoffed. "He ordered his valet to watch my door, but the man was more than willing to turn his head for a few bank notes."

Her cousin's glib admission banished what remained of Winifred's fears. Felicity was impulsive and occasionally audacious, but she was still Winifred's best friend. If their family had arranged a trap, Felicity was not involved. All Winifred had to do now was convince Felicity to return home with her.

"Why did the earl not join you on the journey?" Felicity asked.

Winifred's knee had started bouncing again. She pressed her heel firmly to the ground. She'd carefully avoided mentioning Marcus's condition in her letters to her cousin, but it seemed now was the chance to reveal all. Given Felicity's interest in the occult, she might have some insight into the "mate atrophy" Marcus had mentioned.

"My lord rarely ventures away from the castle," Winifred said, choosing her words with care. This was a topic that could ignite rumors.

Felicity's eyebrow rose. "I see. Well, I cannot say I miss his absence, if it means I have you to myself. It feels as if we are girls again."

Winifred smiled. Indeed, spending time with Felicity reminded her of how they'd gotten along like siblings when they'd been younger, before her parents had spirited her out of the country.

"Do you remember that night?" Winifred whispered. "When our uncle…" She touched her bodice above where the scar rested. She would never forget trembling with fear as Vincent held her firmly from behind while her uncle had approached, wielding the branding iron. The scream that had ripped out of her throat when it had touched her flesh had seemed more animal than human. "I cannot imagine what it is like continuing to live in that house after what he did to us." She met Felicity's gaze. "Come home with me, Fel. You could be free of him."

"I cannot," Felicity said. "Please don't ask to explain, Winnie." Then she brushed a feather that had drooped over the edge of her straw hat back into place and continued in a much lighter tone. "Living with Uncle Ethan is not without its challenges. But tell me more about the earl."

Something was wrong. It was typical of her cousin to abruptly change the topic, but not like this. It had to have been their uncle. Maybe Felicity feared he had more spies watching them. If so, it was best for Winifred to proceed as she always did with her cousin and let the matter drop. She would get answers from Felicity later, in a more private setting.

"He has exceeded my expectations in every regard," Winifred said.

"I am glad to hear that." Felicity picked up a spoon. "I admit I had my concerns. The earl's ancestors and ours have a… complicated history."

The way her cousin carefully chose her words made Winifred wonder if Felicity already knew about Marcus's nature. It shouldn't have been a surprise. Thanks to her mother, Winifred's education in her family's history had ended the night of the branding, but Felicity had not been so blessed. If Marcus was right and the stories she'd been told as a girl were true, then had Felicity known Marcus was a vampire since before the wedding? That would explain her whispered warnings and dire predictions.

Was her cousin a hunter?

She shivered. Felicity had been her first and only friend for most of their lives. It pained Winifred to think Felicity might have kept such a significant secret. At the same time, she simply could not believe Felicity meant her harm. They had been through too much together. Spies or no, Winifred had to get Felicity to talk.

"What do you know of the Devilles?" Winifred asked.

Felicity tapped her spoon on the table. "Not much. The title is relatively new." She sniffed. "But as our uncle said, our family has a feud with theirs."

That was quite enough speaking in circles for Winifred. She picked up a piece of shortbread, nibbled the edge, then said, "I wouldn't call one family hunting the other like animals a mere 'feud.'"

Felicity's hands jerked, causing her to slosh tea onto the table. She grabbed a napkin and dabbed at the spill. "What did the earl tell you?"

Winifred picked up her saucer so Felicity could wipe beneath it. "Everything I needed to know. As his wife, I tend to my husband's needs. *All* of them."

Felicity wrapped her ice-cold fingers around Winifred's wrist. "Does he know about our family history?"

Winifred twisted out of her cousin's grip. "That is none of your concern."

She'd intended to convince her cousin to return to the castle with her, but now that she knew Felicity had known the truth all along but had elected not to tell her, she wasn't sure that was a good idea.

What other secrets was her cousin keeping?

"You cannot allow him to bite you, Winnie," Felicity said. "He is a creature of pure evil. I had thought you would be safe as his wife, but—"

"Fel!" Winifred regretted bringing up the topic in such a public venue. "Marcus is a gentleman."

They had not been married long, but the letters they had shared had laid the groundwork for their relationship. He had his flaws, but he wasn't cruel and certainly not *evil*.

Felicity narrowed her eyes. "They are monsters, Winifred, and not to be trusted." She straightened. "But we should not discuss this here. Let's go to the museum. There's something I must show you."

Winifred shifted in her seat. "I agree." It was suddenly much too crowded. She'd started the day intending to discover what was so important that Felicity had called her away and then convince her cousin to return with her, but now all she wanted to do was change Felicity's mind.

It wasn't too late. She'd indulge Felicity's request for a museum visit and then try again.

The next hour passed in awkward silence as they found a cab and crept through the morning traffic. The cramped confines made Winifred sweat beneath her walking dress, and the quiet was almost oppressive, but she did not dare raise the topic of Marcus again while their driver could overhear. Instead, she chewed the inside of her cheek until they arrived at their destination and exited the cab.

The street outside the museum was packed, forcing Winifred and Felicity to walk arm-in-arm until they reached the entrance. After paying for tickets, Felicity urged Winifred through the crowd.

Inside it was nearly the same temperature as outside, but much less humid. Winifred hardly noticed, however, as her attention was immediately drawn to the many Greek statues dotting the open space. They were marble, and several had rugged stumps where their heads had once rested. The ones that did not, however, seemed to stare at her with sightless eyes.

"The relics are tucked in a small room at the very back," Felicity said. "Follow me."

Winifred shifted on her feet. "'Relics'?"

"They are the reason I needed you to come to Glasgow. It is better you see them before we discuss your husband further." She started walking away, forcing Winifred to run to catch up.

"Most of the relics were found in Rome," Felicity said, in the crisp tones of a woman used to giving speeches. "The 'Winston cache,' as it is now known, is the largest collection of vampiric artifacts ever discovered."

Winifred's shoes squeaked on the marble tile as she missed a step. "Did you say *vampiric* artifacts?"

"Yes," Felicity said without stopping. "It has been difficult to find a museum to agree to display them, as you might imagine." Her cousin turned a corner and entered a dark room. When

Winifred joined her, what she saw inside made her jaw drop open. There was an enormous closed casket leaning against the wall, a framed sketch of a hulking creature that could only have been a werewolf, and crosses hanging from nails driven into the walls.

Felicity caressed the edge of the casket. "The vampire trap is my favorite. It can hold as many as three vampires and the wood was soaked in a particular blend of herbs designed to mimic the effect of sunlight." She rubbed a spot with her sleeve. "This is only one of several I've helped restore. Uncle Ethan says there is a spell on them that makes them irresistible to vampires."

"That's barbaric," Winifred whispered. She wasn't sure which was worse; that she couldn't stop imagining Marcus screaming as he was shoved into the casket, or that in her imagination, her cousin was the one doing the shoving.

Felicity's smile widened. "Our family has spent decades gathering these treasures. Which you would know if your mother hadn't taken you to Toronto. Individually, they would present as mere curiosities, but together..." She inhaled sharply. "Well, I hope it is enough to convince some to reconsider their beliefs. And if your husband's nest decides that makes me too dangerous to be allowed to live... Well." She sniffed. "At least I will have tried."

Winifred felt like a fox that had dismissed a shining, silver circle on the forest floor as unimportant until metal teeth closed around her leg. She'd underestimated her cousin. "You don't mean that."

Marcus might be furious when he learned of Felicity's actions, but he was no killer. Not anymore. The remorse he'd expressed about the lives he'd taken made that obvious.

That was when Winifred spotted the small portrait nestled among a collection of others. She stepped forward with numb hands until she was close enough to make out the detail of the face in the daguerreotype. Within seconds, she knew it was Marcus. If she could recognize him, surely others would as well.

He had not been out in society for a decade, but there would still be people who remembered his face.

"You can't do this," Winifred said before she could think about what she was doing. She turned to her cousin. "If anyone learns you donated the items for this exhibit, they will think you are mad."

Felicity's expression shuttered. "My reputation is of little concern. If I can convince a single person of the danger that lurks in the shadows, it will be worth it."

"Why?" Winifred asked. "Why do all of this? What has Marcus done to you?"

Felicity blinked several times. "'Marcus'?" She uttered a sharp laugh. "He is but one of many of the evil creatures that lurk in this city and around the world."

"I don't understand," Winifred whispered. She didn't recognize the bitter woman in front of her.

Felicity closed her eyes and seemed to wilt. "Four years ago, when I was an innocent girl... I watched a vampire murder my parents."

Winifred had to grasp the edge of a table to keep from falling over. "M-My mother said your parents died in a carriage accident."

Felicity scoffed. "A clever lie. Why do you think she uprooted your family? It was not because of the initiation. Our uncle told me everything. Aunt Margaret fled because she was afraid she'd suffer the same fate as my parents."

As awful as it was, it made sense. Winifred had always found it odd that her mother had continued to insist she learn about their family history, even though she'd claimed they had relocated to Toronto to get Winifred away from her "barbaric relatives."

"Now you know why I was concerned about your marriage." Felicity clasped Winifred's hands. "Your husband might seem kind, but he is a murderer. They all are."

The conviction in her cousin's voice shook Winifred to the

core. She knew he'd done terrible things, but she'd never have used the word *murderer* to describe him. He was a predator and humans were his prey. "You're wrong."

Felicity pursed her lips. "You need more proof. I understand." She dragged Winifred deeper into the room and picked up a book. It had to be at least a hundred years old, judging from the metal clasps and tooling on the leather cover.

"This book lists suspicious deaths recorded by our family," Felicity said. She flipped through the pages, then turned the book around and held it out so Winifred could see. "Look for yourself."

Winifred leaned forward and read the page. Each entry contained a brief description of each human's age and occupation, followed by Marcus's name. Not once or twice, but hundreds of times.

Felicity flipped the page. The entries continued, each with Marcus listed.

"This means nothing," Winifred said, even though it felt like the floor were lifting and heaving beneath her. Seeing the list of names made it more difficult to think of Marcus's victims as prey.

But even if Marcus had killed them, he'd changed. He wasn't the same person who had snuffed out all those innocent lives.

"You don't know him," Winifred said. "Come to the castle. Talk to him. Then you'll understand." She could still fix things.

Felicity chuckled. "It's too late for that."

Winifred's heart dropped into her stomach. "What do you mean?"

Felicity's eyes were cold. "As we speak, Vincent is taking care of the problem. Soon the world will have one less vampire."

Chapter Thirty

MARCUS PROWLED THE halls like a caged animal. He'd tried reading, but his mind refused to focus, and pacing was proving equally futile. It had been less than a day, but he ached as if something vital had been ripped out of him. He couldn't stop thinking about Winifred. Was she safe? Did she miss him as much as he missed her? Were Jonathan, Cordon, and Kitty watching over her properly? Why hadn't any of them returned with news?

Sending them all had been a mistake. If he'd ordered Cordon to remain behind, he could have relied on his brother's mental bond with Kitty to relay information back from Glasgow.

He climbed the steps to his tower. Working would at least distract from the pain in his heart. It was better than stalking the castle and frightening the maids.

But when he reached the top of the steps, his legs burned and there was a crackling in his lungs. He stumbled to the window and cranked it open. The cool air flowing over his skin provided some relief, although a dampness beneath his shirt suggested he'd aggravated his sores.

As he looked out over his land, he noticed a gathering of cows in the pasture. There was something on the ground, a pile of what appeared to be turnips. That was odd, as he had instructed his staff to feed them only grass and hay.

He put his hands on the windowsill and felt a punch. He'd sliced his thumb on a sliver of wood. The wound did not heal right away but oozed dark-red blood. It was nearly identical to the cut Winifred had sustained in his workshop on their wedding night. He brought the digit to his mouth and nearly gagged at the sour taste. It was the same flavor he'd noticed in his tainted samples. That meant whatever had infected his livestock was still affecting him. It seemed impossible, given he'd only drunk from wild-caught animals, his valet, and his wife since discovering the contamination, but there was one way to know for sure. Especially now that the thicker glass he'd commissioned had finally arrived.

He used the sharp edge of a knife to slice his upper arm and when he'd collected enough for a sample, placed it in the device.

The gears spun smoothly as he cranked. He counted in his head for two minutes, then opened the lid and removed the vial. The layers were much more distinct, although the topmost one was frustratingly pink.

A gentle rap at the door interrupted his thoughts. "Enter."

"You have a guest," his butler said. "Mr. Ethan Sorrow wishes to speak with you."

There was a stranger inside his home. A hunter. Marcus felt like worms were burying their way through his flesh. Now that Winifred was gone and his affliction had made him as weak as a fledgling, they were staging their attack. He would never get to tell Winifred how much he cared or discover if she was his fated mate. She'd return from Glasgow to find his decapitated corpse hanging from the ramparts.

A familiar tingling started in his fingertips. This sample slipped out of his hand. His nerves were getting the best of him again.

One, two, three… Inhale. *Four, five, six…* Exhale.

It took a few attempts, but eventually, the tightness in his chest eased and logic reasserted itself. If the hunters wanted him dead, they would not have announced themselves. This must be something else. Possibly regarding Winifred. If she'd been taken hostage, the hunters might have prepared a list of demands.

He burst into movement, stopping only when he'd reached

the receiving room. There was a man waiting dressed entirely in black, with an unusual, triangular-shaped hat perched atop his head.

Outside, a wolf let out a plaintive howl.

Marcus took a deep breath, then walked forward. "Good afternoon."

The man spun around and reached into his jacket before slowly lowering his hand.

"My lord," he said. "I am Winifred's uncle, Mr. Ethan Sorrow."

It was at that moment that Marcus recognized the gold-tipped cane clutched in the man's hand. He was the heckler from the symposium. The man who had triggered his first attack.

"No," Marcus whispered. He didn't want to believe the evidence before his own eyes because if it was true, then this was another of his failures. If he'd done his duty after the wedding and joined his guests, he would have seen and recognized the man then.

Mr. Sorrow grimaced. "I see you remember me." He lifted his cane. "It was a strategic decision, attending that event and pretending to be one of your kind. Given that it brought you here, I will not apologize."

Marcus wanted to strangle the man, but doing so would only bring more hunters. He cleared his throat. "To what do I owe the pleasure of this visit?"

He would not mention Winifred's trip in case he was wrong, and she was safe in Glasgow under the watchful guard of his brothers.

But what if they'd been captured, too?

Mr. Sorrow inclined his head. "I did not come to see my niece, if that is what you are wondering. My ward is seeing to Winifred's... education. When Felicity reveals the extent of your bloody past, Winifred will never want to return here. As to the other members of your nest..." He shrugged. "The vampire traps we left near their daylight resting places were more than enough to subdue them. I expect they'll escape eventually, but by then, it will be too late."

The wriggling worm sensation in Marcus's chest returned. That explained why none of his nest siblings had returned with news. They were trapped in wooden caskets, likely screaming in agony as the herbs infused in the traps burned their skin as effectively as sunlight. Cordon and Jonathan were strong enough that they'd escape on their own, in time, but Marcus could only pray Winifred had not been caught.

If the hunters had tortured Cordon's mate, they wouldn't live long to regret it.

The only thing that kept Marcus from throttling Mr. Sorrow was the knowledge that the man had underestimated Winifred. She might be devastated to learn her beloved cousin wasn't innocent, but he trusted she would not be so easily turned against him.

Mrs. Gillanders entered, laid out a tray of biscuits and sweets, curtseyed, then twisted the fabric of her black skirt in her hands.

"That will be all, Mrs. Gillanders," Marcus said.

Her forehead wrinkled, but she left.

That was when he noticed the sky outside the window had taken on a deep orange hue. It was a color he recognized from more than a century earlier when he'd clung to a broken chunk of mast in freezing water as violent winds had fanned the flames consuming what had once been his ship.

"What have you done?" he whispered.

Mr. Sorrow chuckled. "An unfortunate accident with a lantern in a barn on the edge of the village. I am afraid your staff will soon be drawn away to help fight the fire."

It appeared the hunters had thought of everything. Marcus clenched his jaw and gestured to the two couches in the center of the room.

"I will be frank, my lord," Mr. Sorrow said, when they were alone. "I would prefer not to fight."

Marcus felt his eyebrows rise. It was an extraordinarily rude way to begin a conversation, but he would not rise to the bait. He was married to Winifred and there was little her family could do about it.

Aside from murdering him.

"However," Mr. Sorrow continued, "I cannot allow my niece to remain here unless I know you are taking proper care of her."

Marcus resisted the urge to snort. He'd already suspected Mr. Sorrow was holding Winifred hostage, but now he was certain. If her uncle had cared about her wellbeing, he would have attended the wedding ceremony. Instead, he'd appeared only long enough to upset Winifred with his fictional claim of a 'feud.'

"Tell me what you want," Marcus said.

Mr. Sorrow leaned forward. "I propose a truce. If you give me your word she will not become a vampire, I will withdraw my hunters and guarantee we will not pursue your nest."

Some of the tension drained from Marcus's body. Was that all the hunters wanted? "I assure you, she is happy, and I have no intention of making her a vampire."

"I am glad to hear that." Mr. Sorrow said. He picked up a treat from the tray. "Candied turnip. How creative."

Turnips again. He'd been seeing them all over his property. "I believe we have a surplus."

"Interesting." Mr. Sorrow turned the treat around with his fingers. "Do you know what happens to livestock that eat too many vegetables from the *Brassica* family?"

Marcus shook his head. He relied on his groundkeeper for such knowledge.

"They weaken until the farmer has to put them out of their misery." He put the dessert down. "And now that I have stalled long enough to ensure none of your staff will come running to your rescue, I can confirm it is precisely what we intend to do to you, my lord."

Marcus felt like a bucket of cold water had been dumped over his head. Turnips. Countless hours spent in his workshop trying to find the source of the contamination and the answer was so simple. It was almost as embarrassing as having a hunter be the one to tell him.

But before he could decide how to respond to the threat, the window shattered, and an enormous silver wolf leaped into the room.

Chapter Thirty-One

TWO HOURS INTO the carriage ride, Winifred's pulse pounded in the back of her neck. Keenan snored gently, having slept through most of the journey. Winifred wished she could have done the same, but she hadn't been the one who had frantically packed the trunks after Winifred had returned from the museum in a panic. Keenan had been curious, of course, but Winifred had been too upset to provide an explanation beyond a strong desire to return home.

She put her head in her hands. She couldn't lose Marcus. It would be like tearing out a piece of heart she hadn't realized she'd been missing until she'd met him. Never had she thought Felicity could be so cruel. It was as if her cousin had carved an image of Marcus in her mind that was centuries old and refused to recognize that he might have changed, which was absurd. Before Winifred had forced him to confess, he'd admitted that he hadn't even drunk from humans in centuries. It made her wonder what other vampires were like to make her family so determined to eradicate them.

She recalled the book of names Felicity had shown her. Once, she would have said that written history was unchangeable, albeit subject to the interpretation of the reader. That belief had been naïve. She'd been so focused on the past, she'd failed to see her own biases. Humanity changed and evolved. She could never truly understand who Marcus had been because that person no longer existed. The best she could do was rewrite the narrative to better reflect who he had become.

She peered out the window and spotted billowing smoke in the distance. As they ascended a hill, she saw a line of people passing buckets of water toward a burning building. Several of the figures worked in the castle. She was briefly tempted to tell the driver to stop—there had to be some way she could help, even by tearing sheets into bandages—but then she realized what the fire meant.

The castle would be nearly empty, perfect for an ambush.

Her stomach gurgled as a horrifying image swam to life in her mind. Her uncle would find Marcus sleeping and stab a dagger into his chest. It would be over in seconds, and Marcus would never know how much she loved him. She gritted her teeth and tried to banish the premonition by staring at the tiny shape of the castle in the distance. The full moon sat high above it, faintly visible through the clouds.

When that failed to eradicate the awful vision, she imagined herself stepping between her husband and uncle with her arms spread. The cold metal would cut through her twill walking suit as if it were gossamer, then slide between her ribs and pierce her heart.

She clutched her sides and gasped. She could almost feel her lungs crackling as they filled with blood. There would be nothing left of her but a writhing, gurgling shape at her uncle's feet.

The carriage hit a rut, making her bottom leave the seat and thrusting her back into the present. No matter how vivid her thoughts were, they were nothing more than a product of her terrified mind. She braced herself against the walls and remembered what she'd told Marcus before she'd left for Glasgow. She had been, and still was, prepared to become a vampire. They could remain together forever, and she could experience history rather than reading about it in dusty tomes. It would mean giving up the sun, her mortal life, and her uncaring family, but those were trifles compared to the thought of losing him. Even thinking such dire things made her feel like she'd already taken her uncle's dagger through her ribs.

The carriage slowed to a stop. Keenan jolted awake and yawned. "Have we arrived?"

"Yes," Winifred said. Then before Keenan or anyone else could open the door, she gathered her skirts and raced up the stone path. The exterior entrance to the castle was devoid of footmen, but she did not let that stop her. She grasped a brass ring and heaved until there was enough space to squeeze inside. When she popped through, she yanked the hem of her dress free from where it had caught and looked around.

The foyer was silent. There should have been servants bustling about, but she couldn't hear footfalls upstairs or smell the garlic cheddar scones Mrs. Grange baked every morning. They must have all left to help with the fire.

She inhaled deeply, then shouted. "Marcus!"

Her own voice came back to her in a mocking refrain.

Marcus, Marcus, Marcus…

She didn't have time to search. Her uncle was likely already preparing to execute her husband. As it was past sunrise, the most logical place for him to be was in his bedchamber. She was about to ascend the stairs when she felt an odd sensation in her head, like someone had wrapped a string around her brain and tugged.

The red receiving room.

The thought popped into her head, unbidden. She didn't stop to wonder how it had happened but lifted her skirts and made her way to the third floor, then down the hall until she arrived at a scene out of a horror novel.

The furniture had been overturned, the walls were splattered with blood, and Marcus stood with one hand clasped to his waist, panting heavily. His hair was plastered to his head, the arm of his coat was torn off, and there were deep gashes all over his body.

Uncle Ethan was nowhere to be seen, but when she saw the only other occupant of the room, she shrieked. An impossibly large four-legged creature swiveled its head until black eyes bored into hers. Saliva dripped from its open jaws and formed smoking puddles on the floor. The creature writhed and twisted, shrinking until it was only her bloodied, naked cousin.

Vincent was a werewolf.

That explained why he'd loathed her father's hunting dogs and his wretched need to possess her as a wolf might claim a mate.

Come to me.

Those were Marcus's words, but he hadn't spoken. She was running to him before she realized it. When he took her hands, something sparked between them, like static, and her mind opened. There were no other words to describe it. One moment she was alone in her head, and the next, she wasn't. She felt him reach for her, mentally, and met him with an exuberant sharing of sensation. She could feel her own hands clasping him because his body was hers. They were one and the same. She physically and mentally embraced him, passing along every reassuring feeling she possessed. He sent back a powerful wave of love that warmed her from the inside out.

"I can feel you," she whispered.

The ragged edges of his thoughts scraped against hers. She gently pulled back, just enough that she could distinguish where she ended and he began. He must have felt the same, as he blinked several times, like he'd been spun around in circles.

Vincent stood from behind the couch and scowled fiercely. "You cannot support that monster, Winifred." He held out his arms. "Come with me and I will bring you home, away from this nightmare."

She slid her hand into Marcus's. "*This* is my home."

Vincent picked up a pistol from the ground and leveled it at Marcus. "Then you have made your decision."

There was a loud bang, and a bullet struck Marcus in the torso. The pain reverberated through her body. She clasped her own shoulder, expecting to feel carnage, but there was nothing there.

Marcus toppled over. She shrieked his name and clawed at his shirt. The edges of the bullet wound weren't knitting together.

"No," she whispered. She brought her wrist to his lips. "Bite me."

His head lolled to the side.

"Marcus!" Her voice broke. "I can't lose you." She wiped his face with the corner of her sleeve. The fabric of his coat was mangled, and the angry flesh beneath torn to shreds and speckled with bits of metal. She picked them off while tears flowed down her cheeks and splattered on his face.

His eyelid fluttered open. "Winifred. I have seen to it… You will be… taken care of. Your uncle…" He trailed off and went limp.

A sob burst from her mouth. It felt as if someone had taken a sword and ran it through her heart, then pulled it out, leaving her with a gaping hole in her chest.

A hand landed on her shoulder. "Leave him."

She shrugged away from Vincent and ran her hands over Marcus's body, searching for a knife or dagger or anything with a sharp edge. If he was not conscious enough to bite her, she would have to help him.

"Winifred, that's enough," Vincent said. "Do you know what I've done for you? I've spent the last several months setting everything in motion to earn your freedom. Now we can finally be together."

She heard his words but didn't care. Her arms trembled from the effort of holding Marcus. His skin was slippery, but she couldn't give up. The moment she did, it would be admitting that he was gone.

"We have to leave," her cousin said. "Your husband's distress will summon more of his kind."

Vincent was going to take her away. Marcus would die, cold and alone, while her family forced her back to Canada. She would live the rest of her life with a piece of her soul missing.

It was not a life she would accept.

Her numb fingers grasped the ground until they landed on a

shard of glass. She curled her fingers around it and when her cousin crouched, she slashed.

He leaped out of the way but sustained a thin scratch along his arm. Blood splattered to the ground. "You cut me!" He snarled, and his skull elongated. In moments, he'd become a wolf again. She wouldn't get another chance. She brought the shard to her neck and sliced. The pain was intense, but she gritted her teeth to keep from crying out and she leaned over Marcus.

Drink.

Her vision grew hazy. Vincent was shouting, but she couldn't make out the words over the *whooshing* in her head. She clung to Marcus until her strength gave out, then closed her eyes and fell on top of him.

At least they would die together.

Lips moved against her neck, followed by two sharp pokes.

Pleasure coursed through the bond, wrapping her in a glowing, golden haze. She could feel her vital essence leaving her body and entering Marcus, restoring his strength and healing the damage he'd sustained.

She brought her fingers to his shoulder and felt firm, cold skin. "Thank God."

He kissed her forehead. "I would never leave you."

She buried her face in his shirt, even though it was crusty and smelled like sweat. Nothing else mattered except that they were together.

"Don't let that monster confuse you," Vincent said. "You belong to me, Winifred."

"There is only one monster in this room," Winifred said. "And it's not my husband."

Marcus's amusement filtered through the bond, but when he looked at Vincent, his voice was full of menace.

"It's time for you to leave."

"I'm not going anywhere without her," Vincent said.

She felt Marcus's white-hot anger. He would kill anyone who came between them, and she didn't care. So much had changed since they'd met.

He gently positioned her against the wall. She had only enough strength to remain sitting, propped up by the stiff fabric of her gown and her corset. It was distinctly odd watching passively as Marcus faced off against a man she'd once considered family.

Vincent's body expanded with a sickening crunch. Silver fur erupted from his skin. He fell onto his hands and knees and growled like a beast.

"This is your last chance," Marcus said. "If you do not leave now, you will be removed from this castle in pieces." He flicked his arm, and an enormous ruby blade materialized. It was like nothing she'd ever seen, somehow liquid and solid at the same time.

"I really do not want to kill you," Marcus said. "I know what was done to you was not your choice."

Vincent opened his jaws, bearing razor-sharp teeth.

The golden thread in Winifred's mind pulsed so strongly that it reverberated throughout her entire body.

Marcus lurched. He was so fast that in the time it took for Winifred to blink, he had gone from standing in front of her to across the room with his hand buried in Vincent's fur and the shimmering blade pressed against her cousin's neck. Then there was a wet tearing sound, and the beast toppled over... without his head.

Chapter Thirty-Two

MARCUS CARRIED WINIFRED in his arms through the empty halls. She was too silent, yet he could feel her on several levels. The moisture on her warm skin. Her faintly soapy scent. The pressure of his own arms wrapped around her. If he paid too much attention, the looping of sensation between them made him dizzy.

"I can't..." She shook her head. "It's too much."

Her distress buzzed against his mind, but as he welcomed her physical touch, he welcomed the sound of her thoughts and the feel of her emotions. It was like coming home after being marooned in a sea of despair. The bond between them had filled cracks in his heart he hadn't even realized had been there. Even after mere minutes, he knew he would not survive losing the connection.

They reached her room, and he heard shouting from elsewhere in the castle. It could have been his staff, or Mr. Sorrow. He'd lost track of the hunter with the arrival of the wolf.

He juggled Winifred in his arms, opened her door, then deposited her on the bed. She'd done everything she could. Now it was his turn to rescue his brothers and Kitty. He closed his eyes and concentrated on the faint sparks of their presence. They were close. On the grounds. Likely engaged with other hunters in combat.

He reached the top of the entry staircase. Two people in black cloaks argued in the entryway. Winifred's uncle, who had raced out of the receiving room when his nephew had attacked, shook his head as Winifred's cousin Felicity Sorrow gestured with her arms, obviously making an impassioned plea.

"Leave," Marcus said, pitching his voice so it carried.

The figures sprang apart before facing him, shoulder to shoulder. The old man wasn't a problem. But he was not keen on taking the life of a woman, especially one who was friends with Winifred.

"Miss Sorrow," he said.

She straightened. "Do not use my name, vampire! Where is Vincent? What have you done with my brother?"

He crossed his arms. "The werewolf is dead. I suggest the rest of you leave before you end up the same. There has been too much blood shed this night already."

Mr. Sorrow slashed his arm through the air. "Absolutely not. You might have survived our first assault, vampire, but I am not afraid of you, nor of death. I will do whatever is necessary to avenge my nephew and see every wretched person living in this castle executed."

Miss Sorrow grabbed his arm. "Uncle, no! The staff are innocent."

"They are complicit, for serving a monster. We cannot suffer them, or my turncoat niece, to live."

"Please, Uncle—"

Mr. Sorrow slapped Miss Sorrow, sending her sprawling to the ground. She clutched her cheek and whimpered.

Marcus had seen enough. He descended the steps one at a time while sending a thread of power to all the blood Vincent had spilled in his reckless assault. It came at his call, dripping from the ceiling like rain and drenching the hunters. With the steady, reassuring beacon of Winifred in his mind, he felt ready to take on an army. A few measly humans were no threat.

Miss Sorrow rose unsteadily to her feet and wiped her face with a handkerchief, turning the white cotton bright red. "This isn't right, Uncle. We should leave. We can't win this fight."

The old man shoved his niece behind him. "Let me handle this, child."

Pity. He should have listened.

Marcus willed his strength into his blood. As it crept from his body, a throbbing started between his temples, but still he continued, until a pool formed beneath the intruders. They didn't even seem to notice they'd walked directly into a trap.

"I will give you one last chance," he said. The red liquid coiled beneath their feet. If they agreed to leave, he would summon it back. But if they refused, he would show them what a two-century-old vampire could do.

"I-I don't want to die here." Miss Sorrow backed up, slipped, and fell on her rear. He stared at her as she scrambled upright, then turned around and fled. He would have to deal with her another time, but for the moment, he would let her go.

Mr. Sorrow slid his hand into his cloak, likely reaching for this revolver. Before he could wrap his fingers around the hilt, a scarlet tree sprouted from the floor, skewering him in dozens of places and lifting his limp body to the ceiling. He gurgled and flailed before finally falling silent. The tree formed tiny buds that flowered and released a shower of bloody petals.

Marcus recalled his power. His victim remained floating in the air for a fraction of a second before splashing into the crimson pool in a lifeless heap.

The ache in Marcus's head eased, and his legs gave out. He grasped the railing to keep from falling down the steps.

It was over.

He reached reflexively for Winifred's mental presence. As long as he had her, he would never return to that awful darkness that had made him want to walk into the sun and sunder himself into a pile of ash.

I'm coming.

He pushed the words through their bond but didn't know if she'd heard. Their mating was still too new. There were many things he was still learning about how it worked.

He would have to consult with Cordon.

He turned the last corner that led to Winifred's room, when a figure barreled toward him and hit him square in the stomach. It took several seconds to realize it was Miss Sorrow holding her brother's severed head against her chest. She shoved him and Marcus hit the window at the end of the hallway with a *thud*.

"Demon!" she cried. She removed a pistol from under her cloak, but the tears streaming down her face made Marcus doubt she would pull the trigger.

"I did not want to kill him," he said. "I know what it's like to be changed into something against your will."

He didn't need to ask to understand Vincent hadn't wanted to become a werewolf. There had long been stories of hunters using other creatures to assist them in their patrols.

"Did your uncle do it?" Marcus asked. "Did he lock your brother in a cell with an infected human and let it happen, turn his own blood into a weapon?"

Miss Sorrow's lips thinned. "Nothing you say will convince me you aren't evil." Then she screwed her eyes shut and fired. There was a sharp report, followed by the sound of shattering glass. Miss Sorrow had swung her arm up, missing him. He glanced at the broken hallway window behind him, then back at her, and at the pale figure approaching her from behind.

Winifred, stay away from her.

His wife shook her head. He could feel her determination and her love for the woman standing between them.

Miss Sorrow's eyes were enormous, and her arms were shaking. As if sensing Winifred's presence, she glanced over her shoulder, then dropped her brother's head. "Winnie! You're hurt."

Winifred limped the remaining distance and draped herself over her cousin. Miss Sorrow returned the embrace, causing Winifred to wince.

Be careful, dearest.

He would refrain from harming Miss Sorrow because Winifred cared for her, but if Miss Sorrow made any movements that might suggest Winifred was in danger, Marcus would sever the connection between the two women by any means necessary.

"Don't do this, Fel," Winifred said. "Marcus isn't your enemy. Vincent attacked us. We had no choice."

Miss Sorrow shuddered, then pulled away from Winifred until she faced both of them, the battle lines drawn.

"You can't stay here, Winnie," Miss Sorrow said. Tears dripped down her cheeks. "If you do, I'll never see you again. Losing my brother was difficult enough. I told our uncle not to do it, but he insisted having a werewolf join our cause was the only way to rid the world of vampires. Vincent resisted, but you know Uncle Ethan. He pressured my brother until Vincent gave in."

Winifred fell to her knees with a grunt. Marcus was at her side in an instant, supporting her with an arm around her waist.

"Choose," Miss Sorrow said. "Him or me."

Marcus felt Winifred's decision. A moment later, Miss Sorrow must have realized it, too, because her lower lip trembled.

"We can find another way," Marcus said. He held out his hand but must have startled Miss Sorrow, as she reacted by throwing out her arms. She smacked Winifred, who stumbled out of Marcus's grasp. She pinwheeled her arms. He grabbed for her, but it was too late. Her knees hit the back of the ledge, and she fell backward through the broken window.

Chapter Thirty-Three

*I*T'S NOT YOUR *fault.*

Winifred forced the words through the bond as the horrified expressions on Marcus's and Felicity's faces grew smaller by the second. Air rushed past her, tinged with the acrid stench of smoke. She was falling. Killed by her own cousin.

She wished she could relay the same message to Felicity. Her cousin had acted out of fear, not hatred. That made the betrayal easier to forgive.

She didn't want to die with regrets.

The shock of the impact was so powerful that the air evaporated from her lungs, but it didn't hurt. Maybe that meant she'd been spared and could still make things right with Felicity. She squirmed, but then a powerful throb of pain made her go limp. There was something pinning her in place. She moved her hands to her chest and wrapped her fingers around the narrow shaft of an iron fencepost.

A croaking sound that could have been laughter came out of her mouth. She'd been skewered, just like in the story Marcus had read to her days ago from his journal. History was repeating itself. She lifted her head but was immediately struck by a wave of dizziness that made her stomach gurgle.

"Winifred!"

That was Felicity. Her voice had the hollow softness of someone shouting from a distance. Winifred tried again to move, if for no other reason than to give her cousin some kind of sign that would keep Felicity from falling apart in the days and weeks to come, but her arms and legs no longer obeyed her commands. The best she could do was tilt her head back and forth.

There were other voices, then. She recognized Kitty and Marcus's brother. Marcus was shouting something about fire. It took a few seconds, but then she understood; Marcus was sending them to help the village.

The golden rope in her mind pulsed, blinding her with its intensity. She closed her eyes and shied away from the light, but it smashed through her resistance and sunk its claws into her thoughts.

Hold on, dearest. I'm almost there.

The sick-sour taste of Marcus's fear filled her mouth. She should've been with him, not tethered to a useless lump of flesh. She grabbed for the mental connection, thrashing violently until she wrenched free of her body and flowed through the bond. He was leaping down the steps of the tower three at a time. His hands and feet were numb and there was an awful rattling in his chest, but he didn't slow down until he'd reached the ground floor. Only then did Winifred realize what was happening.

Marcus was caught in the grip of an attack.

She could feel his suffocating panic but was helpless to do anything but watch as he stood before the door to the garden, shaking like the last leaf on a branch in fall, unable to come to the aid of the woman he loved.

A fluttering sensation trickled through the tenuous thread that still tied her to her physical form. He loved her. She ached to hold him in her arms and tell him she felt the same, but her consciousness was fading. She could already feel her body calling her back, even as she stubbornly clung to Marcus.

His knees buckled. He fell but kept one hand clasped tightly around the knob. She could actually see the fear that kept him frozen in place. It was like a sticky, black cobweb clinging to his thoughts. She burned with anger. Marcus did not deserve the suffering that was being thrust upon him. She opened her arms and willed the cobwebs to come to her.

Where she was going, pain was irrelevant.

The clinging tendrils resisted at first but eventually separated from Marcus and drifted to her. She gathered them up, compressed them into a ball, and let it sink into her essence until it vanished.

MARCUS COULDN'T MOVE. It was as if there were a steel mesh draped over him, keeping him pinned in place. Winifred was *dying*, and he was helpless to stop it.

He tried to do as she had taught, breathing and focusing on the present, but awful images kept intruding. Winifred's wide eyes and open mouth as she'd plummeted to the earth. The sickening crunch of her body hitting the fence post. Damp hair falling out of her chignon.

Her human life had ended, but he could still save her, if he could only conquer his fear.

Then a bright light flashed in his mind, and it was as if the weight were being lifted from his body. Not all of it, but enough that he could move. He struggled to his feet, pushed the door open, and raced across the garden to Winifred's side.

Her heart had stopped, but she was not yet gone. He lifted her off the fence post and set her on the ground. Then he brought his wrist to his teeth and bit until his fangs severed his nerves and he could no longer move his fingers. The wound had to be large enough that she would take what she needed before it healed. But when he placed the gash against her lips, she didn't react. He cursed and cupped his mouth around the cut for several seconds, then transferred as much blood as he could to her, forcing it between her lips. She sputtered and coughed. Both were good signs. He took another bite of his arm, this time farther up. Feeding her was a slow process, but he continued until her eyelids fluttered open.

Her irises faded to blue, then turned to pinpoints. She uttered a fierce snarl, and fangs erupted from her jaw. The thin connection between them burst open like a collapsing dam.

She jerked her head toward him. "Did you feel that?"

He touched their foreheads together. "Yes."

She put her hands on his shoulders and struggled to her feet. She tottered like a lamb as he held his arms around her, ready to catch her if she fell.

"I feel so different." She opened her mouth and touched her fangs again. "How do I get them to go back?"

"It's the corpses," he said. "The smell is triggering your new instincts. That's why your eyes are blue, like mine."

She blinked. "My eyes?" Then she smiled. "How fascinating."

She shouldn't have been so pleased to be a vampire, but he didn't begrudge her excitement. The smell of death bothered him as well. If he released control, the vampire in him would bring death to any living creature within reach.

Winifred pushed his arms away and stumbled toward the castle. After a moment of staring at her back, he realized what was happening from the trickle of hunger and desperation coming through their bond. She was a fledgling, and she was hungry. Unless he stopped her, she would find the nearest human and tear out their throat.

She would never forgive herself, or him, if she took a mortal life.

The village was too far away, and he wouldn't subject his staff to a fledgling. There had to be some other way…

His invention. That was their only chance. He caught her just as she picked up speed. She whipped her head around and bared her teeth. An animalistic reaction. Her new body required a fresh infusion.

He grabbed her upper arm and led her to the stairs to his workshop. He couldn't easily bruise her, but he still hated the whimpering sound she made when she squirmed, and he had to tighten his grip.

"We're almost there," he said. "I have what you need in my workshop."

She whimpered. "It hurts, Marcus."

He knew, because he could feel her pain as if it were his own. The gnawing hunger was becoming impossible to ignore. She shouldn't have been so famished, given how much blood she'd consumed, but his poisoned state had likely contributed to her weakness.

They reached the circular room at the top of the tower. He shoved her inside, then bolted the door behind them.

WINIFRED COULD FEEL her own blood pumping through her veins. It was a distinctly odd sensation, like something inside her was trying to claw its way out of her body through her throat. It was made stranger by the sharp pangs assaulting her stomach. She kept licking her lips, but every time she did, her tongue scraped along one of her blasted fangs.

She stared at the glowing orb of the moon, so bright, that it made her eyes burn. This was to be her life now. She would never see the light of day again. She would spend that time asleep or do whatever vampires did during the day.

Marcus would know. He would help her, as she had helped him. They would remain together forever, tied in a way more secure than the piece of paper that declared them married. Now that she knew how to ease his attacks, they could explore the ruins of Pompeii. Visit the site of the Coringa cyclone. Hike up Mount Tambora at night.

The pain in her stomach intensified, making her groan. She knew she was famished, but the thought of eating made her want to cast up her accounts. She turned around and found Marcus slotting a glass vial full of a dark-red substance into the top of his machine. Her mouth watered.

She had to have it.

She lunged, but he was too fast. He caught her around the middle and lifted her into his arms in one smooth motion.

"My blood is tainted," he said as he cranked. "I think that's why you've regressed even faster than most fledglings. I hoped it might be different for mates. But I think I have a solution." The machine creaked and groaned as if it were about to fall apart.

She struggled through the haze in her mind to understand what he was doing. She doubted he could have convinced Smith or another servant to donate so soon after the violence of the fight. They were all likely hiding or had fled the castle.

Marcus released the handle, then removed a vial. Miraculously, the contents were no longer solid red, but divided into fuzzy sections, including dark red and pinkish yellow. He uncapped the glass tube, grabbed a suction device, then siphoned off the top layer and dripped what remained on his tongue. The sour face he made suggested it was not pleasant, but then he grinned.

"It worked."

She swiped for the vial, but again, he was too fast. He scraped the last of the pinkish yellow away, leaving only the red.

"There," he said. "Drink it."

She wrenched it out of his grip and let the contents flow into her mouth. It tasted shockingly bitter but wasn't nearly as foul as she'd expected. It did, however, ease her pain. She scraped the remaining substance with her finger, then stuck the digit in her mouth and sucked.

"How do you feel?" Marcus asked.

She ran her teeth over her tongue. "Better."

He peered into her face with all the seriousness of a physician.

Then she remembered his warning about what happened to newly made vampires and shuddered. "Did I hurt anyone?"

She had only vague memories of the evening. When she tried to bring them into focus, they squirmed out of her grasp.

"You did not," Marcus said. He closed his eyes and visibly

relaxed. "Thank God. It worked."

She screwed up her nose. "You said that before. *What* worked?"

He gestured to her hand. The vial. She hadn't realized she was clinging to it. She pried her fingers apart and let him take it.

"You figured it out." All the time they'd spent practicing, but it had been science that had saved them.

"No. I cannot regret my discovery because we can use it to ease the suffering of unmated vampires and fledglings, but it's not a cure. I set out to find an alternative to mating, but what I found instead was much more precious." He dropped the vial. As it smashed to the floor, he wrapped his arms around her. "I found *you.*"

Chapter Thirty-Four

WINIFRED WAS ALIVE, and his bonded mate.

Marcus buried his nose against her neck and inhaled. Smoky air filled his lungs and made him cough, but he didn't care. The earthy scent of humanity still clung to her skin like droplets of water after exiting a bath, but there were traces of a richer, sweeter aroma, like freshly baked cherry pie.

Her vampire strength was growing.

Her tumultuous emotions washed into his mind. Concern regarding the fire in the village, anger at her cousin's actions, relief that she had survived the attack, curiosity regarding her new powers, and an overwhelming desire to—she cut the connection.

"Your thoughts are too loud," she said. Then she wrenched the stiff collar of his shirt down and ran the tips of her fangs along his chest. A mere scratch, but it shot directly to his cock and made him growl. She was a fledgling but dared to show dominance over her maker.

"Wait." He threaded his fingers in her hair and yanked, forcing her to tilt her head up. "The fire in the village."

Her pupils dilated. "Don't go. I can't… I'm afraid of what I might do if you leave me alone."

He winced at the thought of not helping, but Winifred was right. His place was at her side until she was fully in control of her new abilities and bringing her anywhere near humans would only worsen her cravings. He would have to rely on Jonathan,

Cordon, and Kitty to assist in his place.

The musky scent of his mate's arousal intensified. "Take me, Marcus."

He brought their mouths together and kissed her roughly, spearing his tongue into her mouth so powerfully that she cut him with her fangs. The salty, almost fruity flavor of her blood was the most delicious thing he'd ever tasted. He moved his mouth to her collarbones and licked the smooth area of flesh that had once held her scar. The actual damage inflicted by her family would take much longer to heal, but at least she no longer had to wear her trauma on her flesh.

"Don't hold back," Winifred said as she clawed the few remaining buttons of his shirt. "I want all of you."

He kicked a chair over, grasped her hips, and lifted her onto his desk. Any other night, he would have leisurely peeled each layer of clothing away to build her arousal by denying what she so desperately wanted for as long as possible, but the lust trickling through their bond eroded his patience.

"Faster," she whined.

He channeled his blood into his fingertips, forming razor-sharp ruby claws. He placed the tip of one between her breasts, then swept down in a single smooth motion. Her dress, corset, chemise, and drawers split cleanly in two. She flung the fabric away and reached for him, but he formed his claws into shackles and wrapped them around her wrists.

She wrinkled her nose. "What are these?"

He created a long chain between the shackles and tossed it over a hook in the ceiling, the remnant of a pulley system he'd created months ago but never finished. Then he merged the links until her arms were drawn above her head. When she was fully at his mercy, he shoved the fingers of his left hand between her legs and made her squeal.

"So wet for me," he said. "But are you ready for what comes next?"

She squeezed her legs around his hand. "Yes."

He slapped her arse with his other hand. "Are you sure?"

"God, yes!"

She had suffered enough. He tore off the tattered remains of his clothing and guided the glistening head of his cock to her entrance. At the first touch of her inner lips caressing him, he moaned. Their bond was only open a crack, but he could feel his own cock impaling her as if he were penetrating himself.

"Do you want more?" he asked. "There are other places I could enter you." He spanked her again.

She was breathing so harshly that she could barely speak, but she nodded furiously.

He channeled a thin, thrashing tail out of the end of his spine and used it to snatch a bottle of oil tucked in his desk drawer before winding the appendage around her thigh and down her arse. After properly preparing her rear entrance, he slithered inside her.

"Oh!" She tightened around him and moaned.

He clasped her hips and drew her body up and down on his cock while copying the motion with his tail. Within seconds, her orgasm rippled through the bond and made him come apart. When the throbbing faded, he dissolved her restraints, gathered her in his arms, and carried her back to his bed.

Chapter Thirty-Five

March 7th 1873, Paris

THE STREETS OF Montmartre were quiet, aside from the cooing of nesting doves and the occasional crackle of gas burning in the streetlamps. Winifred tucked herself closer to Marcus's side, exhaling a breath that formed a cloud and vanished over their heads. "Are you sure this is the place?"

Marcus squeezed his hand on her arm. "I am."

The squat building in front of them gave no sign that it was an atelier. It was sandwiched between two other businesses, a restaurant, and a bakery. She wouldn't have even noticed it were it not for Marcus. She'd nearly tripped on her plaid, cotton skirt when he'd come to an abrupt halt at a black door.

"Maybe they have already retired," she said. Not that she was nervous, but that she could feel the trembling of Marcus's arm beneath her fingers. They'd managed many incredible things since she'd become a vampire, but venturing out of the castle long enough to visit his nest siblings in Paris had remained out of reach—until today. His anxiety was growing like a rising tide through their bond. She reached through their minds and wrenched the suffocating tendrils of his anxiety up by the roots until they withered and died. They always grew back, but between her assistance and his exercises, they managed.

Marcus's trembling arm stilled. He nodded. "I am ready."

They walked to the door and opened it, revealing a vibrant interior occupied by two figures. Cordon stood on a pedestal wearing a black-and-orange-checkered suit while Kitty crouched by his feet. There were pins tucked in her mouth and her brow was furrowed.

"Good evening," Winifred said.

Kitty's head whipped toward them. She gasped. Pins fell to the ground. "Winifred! Marcus!" She leaped to her feet and rushed forward.

Winifred met the shorter woman in a tight embrace. "We wanted to surprise you."

Kitty laughed. "You have succeeded. How did you…?" She leaned back and glanced at Marcus, who was clasping arms with a grinning Cordon.

Winifred tapped her temple with her index finger. "We have been practicing."

"Excellent," Kitty said. Then she looked up and down Winifred's body and hissed. "Please do not tell me you have come to my shop wearing readymade clothing."

The despair in her voice made Winifred giggle. "It is all I could manage on short notice."

Kitty shook her head. "No. Absolutely not. You must have a wardrobe befitting a published scholar." She gestured to a set of leather-bound books sitting on a table next to a cast-iron sewing machine. "I have your entire collection." She ushered Winifred down the steps, then stopped her in front of a wall of fabrics. "Does anything call to you?"

Winifred scoffed. "They aren't magic." But before Kitty could respond, she pointed to a lush sapphire velvet. "How about that one?"

Kitty grasped the edge of the bolt and pulled it out. "An excellent choice."

Ten minutes later, Winifred stood on a podium in front of Marcus and Cordon on a chaise while Kitty murmured and walked around her in circles. It was certainly not the way she'd envisioned the evening going, although she probably should have. This was Kitty's place of work. Of course she would not tolerate subpar clothing inside. In fact, if Winifred were honest with herself, she would have admitted she'd chosen the skirt to tweak Kitty's nose.

"Up," Kitty said.

Winifred lifted her arms. "How many items have you completed from your list?"

During one of their previous visits to Scotland, Kitty had told Winifred of the list she'd compiled, of a hundred scandalous activities she wished to complete with her husband, a near-identical copy of the list Cordon had presented her several years prior, before they had married.

Kitty grunted as she ran a measuring tape around Winifred's bust. "Hardly a dozen. *Someone*"—she sent a pointed, disgruntled glance at her husband—"prefers to laze about the shop."

Marcus crossed his legs. "Why am I not surprised?"

Cordon splayed a hand over his chest. "You wound me."

Kitty made a rude sound, then tucked beneath Winifred's arm and tightened the measuring tape. "What about you?" She came to stand in front of Winifred and looked her up and down again. "Have you managed to attend a garden party while you've been in town? A masquerade?"

Winifred shook her head. "Not yet." She would have loved to accept one of the many invitations that arrived for her at the hotel daily, but Marcus wasn't ready. The ruins of Pompeii weren't going anywhere. Her new existence had granted her startling depths of patience.

"What about your parents?" Cordon asked as if he had read her mind.

Winifred sighed. "I've mailed dozens of letters to my mother and cousin but haven't received a single response." After the ambush at the castle, her entire family acted as if she were dead. Were it not for the reports from spies Marcus sent to watch over the hunters, she wouldn't have known that Felicity had taken up a position as an assistant curator at a museum in a small museum in London. Winifred longed to see her cousin in person but was afraid of how Felicity would react when she learned Winifred was a vampire.

At least there hadn't been any more raids on the castle or fires in the village. They had not encountered a single other hunter since that terrible night. But Marcus was still vigilant. She sometimes caught him staring out a window or at a closed door with an unreadable expression, like he was waiting for someone to burst through with weapons raised.

"What have we here?" a voice asked.

Winifred turned her head and grinned. Jonathan, Marcus's youngest brother, leaned against the wall, wearing a black suit and a self-satisfied smirk. His long, black hair was loose around his shoulders and his cravat was untied. If she was not mistaken, there was lipstick smeared on his neck.

"Scoundrel," Marcus said with a grin.

Cordon groaned. "What devilry have you been up to this night, brother? Should I expect a call from a constable?"

Jonathan lifted his eyebrows. "Perhaps." Then he walked over to the sofa where Marcus and Cordon were sitting and sat between them, forcing them apart. He draped his long arms over his brother's shoulders. "What did I miss?"

"Kitty was telling us about her list," Winifred said. That was a much better topic than her family. Thinking about them made her depressed.

"Jonathan does not care about my list," Kitty said. She rolled out the bolt of a velvet on a long, low table. "He is too busy with his curator."

Winifred looked at Jonathan and was surprised to see him blushing. Carefree, unflappable Jonathan. How interesting.

"Tell us about this curator," Winifred said, if only to see how he would respond. She knew Jonathan was a thief and had taken his maker's departure from the nest some more than sixty years ago the hardest, but beyond that, he was an enigma.

"Someone had to watch her," Jonathan said. "She's a danger to the nest."

With a feeling like someone had flicked her forehead, Winifred realized they were talking about her cousin Felicity. The same woman who had barged through the doors to Marcus's castle and had shoved Winifred out a window.

And Jonathan was infatuated with her.

She should have been furious, if only because the wound in her heart that had formed when Felicity had tried to kill both her and Marcus was still raw, but hope stirred in her breast. If anyone could convince Felicity that vampires were not her enemy, it was Jonathan. She only hoped Felicity would not become dangerous to him.

At that thought, she laughed.

Marcus leaned forward. "What is it?"

She shook her head. "I was only thinking about Felicity and Jonathan." She smiled. "My cousin the hunter is involved with a vampire. I don't know whom I should be more worried about."

Jonathan's cheeks turned bright red. "There is nothing going on between Felicity and I, nor will there ever be." Then he crossed his legs and tilted his chin. "I am not like you four. Attach myself to a single woman?" He barked a laugh. "Absolutely not."

Marcus's concern shot through the bond. She responded with gentle reassurance. Jonathan might have been brash and selfish now, but she could sense the loneliness and pain behind his confident words. A time was coming, and she suspected it would be soon, where he would have to face everything he was holding back.

She just hoped he would be ready to accept love when it found him.

About the Author

Melissa lives in Regina, Saskatchewan; the capital city that feels like a small town. A passionate public speaker, board game enthusiast, and lover of all things Halloween, she spends her free time writing and spoiling her two cats.

Website –
melissakendall.ca

Amazon –
amazon.ca/stores/author/B0B8JVQKMC

Facebook –
facebook.com/MAKendallAuthor

Instagram –
instagram.com/makendallauthor

X (Twitter) –
twitter.com/MAKendallAuthor

TikTok –
tiktok.com/@makendallauthor

www.ingramcontent.com/pod-product-compliance
Lightning Source LLC
Chambersburg PA
CBHW060407310726

48976CB00003B/970